LIGHT THE WAY HOME

ELIZABETH ANDREWS

This is a work of fiction. All of the characters, organizations, locations and events portrayed in this novel are products of the author's imagination. Any resemblance to actual events or places or persons, living or dead, is entirely coincidental.

Printed in the United States of America
www.ElizabethAndrewsWrites.com
Cover Design by CK Designs
ISBN 978-1-7346689-0-2 (Paperback)
ISBN 978-1-7346689-1-9 (Ebook)

This story is for everyone who has ever found themselves lost and somehow managed to make their way home, whether home is back where they started, or somewhere new and far away.

And for my husband and my two sons, who have always made sure to light my way home. I love you.

Acknowledgments

I have to thank Cora Lee for spearheading the Common Elements Romance Project, for inviting authors she didn't know to step into her writing world and trusting they could actually pull this off. Huge thanks to her and to all of the other authors who came up with stories to include in the project, all different, yet all tied together-they are a great group. It's been fun, and I hope we do this again!

I need to also thank some of my writing friends for answering questions, for pointing me in the right direction when I needed information or help with something, or just for an ear when I needed one: Holly Bush, Misty Simon, Kelly Metz, Natalie Damschroder, Allison B. Hanson, Susan Meier. You all rock!

Chapter One

Lucie had been on Mac's Light Island for almost three weeks, but the view from the back door of her temporary home still took her breath away. Right now, she realized she'd been standing there staring, slack-jawed, at the sunlight glinting off the grey-blue ocean waves for a good five minutes. Shaking her head, she pulled the door shut and stepped down onto the sidewalk, feeling in her purse for her car keys.

She closed her fingers on the fob as a giggle reached her ears. She turned to the white picket fence that bordered the property next door as a big multi-colored ball sailed over it, toward her. "Oh!" She caught it before it hit her in the face, then started across the grass, balancing the ball on her hand.

Another giggle sounded as she neared the fence, so she adjusted her direction a tiny bit and came to a stop looking directly down onto a tousled blond head.

"I think you lost something," she said.

The little boy's face tipped up quickly, his blue eyes wide with surprise—as if he couldn't believe she'd found him already.

Lucie grinned and held the ball higher.

He smiled as he got to his feet, brushing off his jeans-clad knees.

From seeing him playing outside several times already, she'd guessed he might be four, but now at close range, she scaled that back to three.

"Hi, I'm Hayden," he said, holding out his right hand.

It was her turn to be surprised. She shook his hand, bemused. "Hi, Hayden, I'm Lucie." Not too many three-year-olds had such good manners. Aside from the ball toss at her face, that is. "Nice to meet you."

He glanced up at his ball. "Me an' my dad are your neighbors."

"I see that." She noted he hadn't mentioned his mom. "Who were you playing with?" She gave the ball a little bounce.

"Maybe *you* wanna play with me." Guileless blue eyes locked on her face.

Ah. She squelched the pang in her chest. "I wish I could, but I'm on my way to town. Maybe we can play another time?" she added when his grin vanished.

"Like this afternoon?"

"Hayden!"

The deep voice got her attention–and the boy's–just before a tall, sandy-haired man rounded the back corner of the next-door house.

Lucie's mouth went dry. *Wowza!*

He frowned when he saw them, but his stride never slowed, just changed direction, toward them at the fence. "Hayden, we have to go to Grandma's." He stopped close to the boy. "You were supposed to stay on the porch." His brown gaze lifted to her face. "I'm Nate Baxter." He stuck his right hand out. "Sorry if Hayden bothered you."

She reached across the fence slowly, trying not to gawk at her hot neighbor. "Lucie Russo. And he wasn't bothering me, we were just making a date to play ball." She met his palm and gave a firm shake, pretending not to notice how warm his callused fingers were around hers. Or how wide his shoulders were in the dark flannel shirt.

His brows dipped a little more as he looked from the ball in her hand down to his son. "That isn't nec–"

"I like to play, so it's no problem," she said smoothly, tugging her hand free. "But since you have to go, too," she continued, dropping her gaze to Hayden, "we can do this later, okay?" She held out the ball with a smile.

He grinned as he took it. "Okay. Thanks, Lucie."

She winked, waving as he ran toward his house.

Leaving her with his father, who still didn't look happy.

"You're house-sitting?"

She forced her lips to keep holding the smile. "Sort of. I'm calling it doing a favor for a friend while I have a break."

One of his eyebrows inched up. "A break?"

"My employer relocated my job far away, so I have some free time to help Mindi and Harry while I figure out my next move." Holding the smile now became a real challenge. She hadn't expected to need a back-up for her practical life plan.

He made a small sound, but didn't speak for a moment, his brown eyes staying on her face. "Sorry to hear that," he said finally. "You don't really have to play with Hayden later."

"I try hard not to break promises," she said before he could go any further. "You can check my references with Mindi and Harry if you like."

A ghost of a smile curved his mouth at last. "If they trust you to take care of their place, I already know you're trustworthy."

Lucie swallowed, noting the dimple in his right cheek.

"But I don't want him to intrude if you need to spend your time on a job search."

"I haven't quite reached that part of my break yet. I think I've only reached the shock stage so far." She smiled, pleased with the light, joking tone she'd pulled off. "When I get to acceptance, then I'll have to polish up my résumé."

One of his eyebrows lifted. "Seems like you might be more interested in playing ball in the denial phase, don't you think?"

Lucie laughed at his unexpected tease. "I'll probably need more when I move from bargaining to depression."

Nate smiled, too, and the dimple deepened. "I'm sure Hayden can help you through, if you're sure you don't mind."

"I don't mind at all." She didn't. Having some company might be a good way to stop her brooding.

"Dad! I'm ready!"

Lucie smiled again at his wince.

"I think that bellow is my cue," he said with a crooked grin.

"It was nice to meet you both." She waved and took another step back.

He strode to his house, and she allowed herself to observe--broad shoulders, narrow waist in faded jeans, nice butt, strong legs.

She jerked her attention away from her hot-*temporary*–neighbor. Not where she needed to focus. She took a quick breath and turned to her car parked beside the house. Groceries and mail. That was her purpose this morning. A ferry trip to the mainland, brief contact with the real world, and then back to the island to lick her wounds some more.

———

NATE BUCKLED HIS SON INTO THE BACKSEAT, ONLY HALF-listening to Hayden's chatter. He'd known Harry and Mindi would be away, but he hadn't realized they planned to have someone stay at the house this year, until she'd arrived with two suitcases and many bags of groceries. He glanced up when he heard Lucie back out of the driveway, then drive away.

Hayden never met a stranger, just people he hadn't befriended yet. He suspected his son had employed a little mischief to initiate contact with her, since Nate hadn't noticed her outside since her arrival. Or maybe that was because he spent every waking moment between work, his son and his parents'. And the lighthouse.

He glanced up at the tall structure attached to his house. He had a date with some windows later.

"Daddy, wave to Mr. Micah," Hayden said, sticking one hand out the open door.

Nate waved, too, to humor his son, but he did note the long shadow darkening one of the lighthouse windows. Micah was restless lately. "Okay, Hayden, hands inside the ride."

The boy giggled and clasped his hands in his lap. "Ready!" he shouted, and Nate shut the door.

When he looked up again, the window was shadow-free. He shook his head and slid into the driver's seat of his truck. "Let's get moving, buddy. Grandpa will wonder if we got lost." He started the engine, then headed out of the driveway, turning the opposite direction from where the house-sitter had gone.

In less than ten minutes, he eased to a stop beside his mom's car. She straightened from where she'd been examining a burgundy chrysanthemum, smiling.

"Hi, Gram!" Hayden shouted, waving.

"Inside voice, buddy," Nate said, pushing his door open. "I think you've deafened me."

His son giggled, and then squealed when his grandma opened his door. "Gram! Hi!"

"Hello, young man."

Nate left them and headed for his father's workshop in the backyard. He found Max Baxter bent over a cabinet door, smoothing an oiled rag on the surface.

"Hi, Dad."

The older man glanced up. "Give me a minute. I'm almost done here."

He nodded, but his father had already turned his attention back to his task, so Nate wandered over to where pieces of a birdhouse lay waiting for paint. A foot away, a small table sat upside-down, one broken leg beside it.

"You almost done with that kitchen?" his dad asked.

"Stain's nearly dry, and it'll be ready to load and deliver tomorrow morning." He turned to find his father closing up the oil can.

"I'll give you a hand with that. I think it's going to rain in the afternoon, so you'll want some help."

"Thanks." Nate leaned one hip against the work table. "You sure you don't mind bringing Hayden back? I'll be done with those windows in a couple hours."

"It's fine. It'll give your mom a break from me for a few minutes." He winked.

Nate shook his head. "All right, thanks."

"You got it. Where are they?"

"Probably headed for the kitchen. Isn't that where he always starts?" He pushed upright. "Thanks, Dad."

His father grunted and bent to squint at his door again. "I'll see you later, son."

Nate knew his cues. He pushed the door shut behind him

and waved at his mother, who peered out the kitchen window. She waved, then bent out of sight, most likely to Hayden. He backed the truck from the driveway and steered toward home.

The driveway next door was still empty. Probably gone to the mainland for the day. He parked and looked up at the lighthouse. Time to clean windows. Maybe he could get Micah to give him a hand.

———

LUCIE BREATHED A SIGH OF RELIEF AS SHE LEANED AGAINST the inside of the closed front door. That was too much. She'd only been hiding out like a hermit on the island for three weeks, and already she felt shell-shocked after a few hours with the general public. Holy cow. Now she understood why her friends lived on an island.

Gathering herself, she pushed off the door and carried her bags to the kitchen. Time for a cup of tea and a nap, to recover from the real world. Maybe she'd even drink her tea under the awning out back and nap to the sound of the ocean over the bluff while the weather was nice-ish.

The idea made her smile, and she moved more quickly to put away her purchases. In fifteen minutes, she carried her steaming mug of blackberry tea and a fleece blanket down the back steps to the patio. She'd used the very comfy lounger under the green awning on several warmish mornings to enjoy her breakfast tea at sunrise.

She sank onto it now, setting her mug on the attached side table so she could wrap the blanket around herself. Then she sat back and released a slow breath, her gaze seeking out the blue of the ocean, beyond the spot where the yard became rock.

Just watching the rolling waves relaxed her, the shifting

blues, whites and greys. Lucie reached for her tea and caught a glimpse of movement from the corner of her eye, so she looked up at the lighthouse.

The hot neighbor must be doing double-duty today, cleaning windows at the top of the tall structure. She'd heard the power tools from his cabinet-making business nearly every day, but she hadn't considered that he'd have to care for the connected lighthouse, too.

She watched him stretch to reach the side of a wide pane, then saw the head and shoulders of another man, steadying his ladder. Huh. Maybe his dad. She'd noticed an older couple arrive several times, and the man looked a lot like Nate. Good thing he had help up there. The lighthouse was about five stories high, and a tumble down from the top level would do a lot of damage to a man.

She picked up her mug and turned her gaze back to the ocean. Her trip to the mainland had been productive, even if it had overloaded her system. She had enough groceries now for the next couple of weeks, some new books to read, and she'd stopped at the post office on her way back from the ferry. She could sort out the junk from the actual mail later, maybe over supper. For now a little soothing ocean music to settle her nerves after the unexpected crush of people on the mainland.

Somehow she'd lost track of the days and driven off the ferry into Friday traffic. Judging by the number of people everywhere, a lot of folks were extending their weekends by one day, or otherwise playing hooky to run errands. Too much noise, too many people, every place she'd gone.

She sipped from the mug. It was weird how she'd adjusted to the quiet on the island so quickly–she'd expected to be restless out here. Her job had been in the city, as well as her apartment, which she'd sub-let when she left. It had been years since she'd even lived in a small town.

She'd only been half-joking when she mentioned her grief stages to hot-dad Nate earlier. But she needed to seriously start figuring out what to do with herself when she had to rejoin the real world for longer than a couple of hours at a time. Mindi and Harry would want their house back when their cruise ended, which meant she needed to have her shit—and *a plan*—together by then.

She took another sip of her tea, then glanced over at the sound of a child's voice, followed by a lower rumble.

Hayden ran into his backyard, chattering a mile a minute, then turned to watch an older man coming after him, more slowly. Grandpa.

Lucie frowned, looking up at the lighthouse. Nate must've had another helper.

The childish chatter faded away, and she realized her tea was nearly empty. That meant it was time to think about supper prep. And possibly a foray online to do a cursory search of job sites for ideas. Wrinkling her nose, she got to her feet and finished the last swallow of tea. As she turned to go inside, Nate emerged from the lighthouse's side door, swiping one hand down the side of his jeans. He glanced over and waved at her. She waved back, continuing to the house.

Half an hour later, while sauteeing garlic and onion for soup, she realized he'd exited the lighthouse alone. No helper. Odd.

———

NATE SCHOOLED HIS EXPRESSION TO NEUTRALITY BEFORE turning around. Hayden's chin jutted stubbornly, and his blue eyes narrowed. "I'm saying Lucie might be busy right now," Nate said evenly. "Maybe we'll see her outside tomorrow."

"I can knock on the door." His son crossed his arms on his chest, covering the spotted blue dog graphic. "She said we'd play later, and it's later."

"We can check, but, buddy, you have to promise not to be upset if she's busy. Plus it'll be suppertime soon, so we'll be busy here, too."

Hayden's chin jutted out further.

"Just don't get your hopes up," he said, trying to keep his tone from dropping in defeat.

Hayden bolted for the back door.

Nate followed more slowly, picking up his son's jacket from the chair inside the door. By the time he reached the bottom step, he heard his son's voice, then Lucie spoke in reply, though he couldn't hear the words. When he cleared the lilac bushes, he expected to see Hayden's shoulders droop.

He was a little surprised to see the two of them walking into the middle of the neighboring yard while Lucie bounced the big yellow ball on one hand. Huh. He would've bet on her putting Hayden off. He paused at the open gate between the yards to watch them. They'd stopped, and she crouched in front of Hayden, who chattered a mile a minute. She nodded as she rose.

Hayden jogged backward a few steps, grinning, then held out both hands.

Lucie gave the ball another bounce before she tossed it to him.

His son caught it, giggling. "Too easy," he shouted. He jumped once, then moved a few more steps away from her. "Ready?"

"Ready!" She leaned forward and held out her hands.

Nate wished he could see her expression.

Hayden lobbed the ball at her, and she caught it before it hit her in the face. He smiled and shook his head when his laughing son danced backward a couple more paces. "Throw it again!"

"You sure you can catch it so far away?" The tease in her voice made Nate relax. Lucie Russo might be a nice woman. Mindi and Harry trusted her, which meant she was okay.

But she seemed to be enjoying his son, genuinely enjoying him. Maybe she had nieces or nephews–she was comfortable, chatting with Hayden as they played catch.

He leaned on the fence to watch.

"Daddy, come play with us!"

Lucie straightened and looked over her shoulder, eyes widening.

Nate felt a little kick in his gut at the appealing image–pink cheeks, green eyes that tipped up at the outer corners, full lower lip dropping a tiny bit. Lucie Russo was pretty.

He reined that in as he straightened. He didn't have time for pretty–he had enough on his plate with his son, his business and the lighthouse. Besides, Lucie would be gone as soon as the neighbors returned. "You forgot your jacket, buddy." He held up the red garment by the collar.

Hayden heaved a dramatic sigh, but he ran toward Nate. "All right."

Nate helped him into it, then smiled as the boy rushed back to Lucie, who bent to listen to his chatter, nodding in response.

He started to turn away, then whirled around when the ball hit him square in the back.

Both Hayden and Lucie smiled, and Nate noted the way his son had grabbed her hand. He narrowed his eyes at them, pretending annoyance while he bent to pick up the ball. "Who did that?" he asked gruffly.

They both shrugged and exchanged a sidelong glance.

"Hayden?" He balanced the ball on his fingertips.

His son shrugged again, trying for an innocent expression, but giggling.

"Lucie?"

Her lips twitched, but one of her shoulders lifted in a half-shrug.

Nate considered the pair of them for a few seconds. He bounced the ball once. "Hm," he said finally, palming the ball. "Eeny, meenie, miney–"

Hayden laughed.

"Moe," Nate finished, throwing the ball at Lucie instead of his expectant son.

She caught it, chuckling. "What gave me away?"

"He did." He pointed at his son, who giggled some more. "That giggle is a tell."

"Ah, well, now I know not to play poker with him." She looked down at Hayden. "How far can you catch?"

"Far, far," he claimed and ran across the backyard.

"Really? That far?" She glanced at Nate, who lifted his eyebrows. "Well, let's find out." She threw the ball hard enough to reach the boy, who snagged it before it hit the grass. "Wow, nice catch." She smiled.

Nate watched his son lob the ball, but his little arms couldn't get it all the way back, so he chased after it, then threw it again, this time at Nate, who jogged forward a few steps to catch it. He held it out to Lucie, whose left eyebrow rose. "I have some prep to do if this boy wants supper tonight."

"I actually have a big pot of soup on the stove, if you guys would like to join me." She bit her lip.

"Yes!" Hayden ran over to them. "What kinda soup?"

Nate started to shake his head, then saw his son's happy

expression fall. "It's nice of you to invite us," he said carefully, noting the disappointment that clouded Lucie's eyes before she dropped her gaze. "I don't want to infringe on your space."

Hayden opened his mouth, so Nate cleared his throat.

"But soup sounds really good."

Lucie met his gaze again, startled, and her mouth curved a little. "It should be ready in about ten minutes, so we have time for some more catch." She looked down at Hayden. "And it's chicken corn chowder. I even have bread in the oven to go with it."

His son cheered, jumping up and down and pumping his little fists. "I love hot bread!"

She laughed. "Me, too."

Nate caught himself admiring her smile again and jerked his wayward thoughts back. "So how about you see if you can catch this one, sport?" he said to his son, who raced most of the way across the yard once more.

For ten more minutes, the three of them tossed the ball around, his son laughing and chattering the whole time. Finally, Lucie held her hands up in a T-shape. "I'm going to make sure the soup is really ready, if you guys are hungry."

"Starving!" Hayden shouted, running toward her with the ball.

"Then I can help set the table while someone washes his grubby hands," Nate added.

"Sounds like a plan." She smiled. "Come on in." She led the way to the back door. "There's a powder room around the corner, Hayden, so you can wash up." She gestured as she stepped inside.

Nate steered his son in the right direction, then turned on the light in the small bathroom. "Don't make a mess, buddy. Just clean hands, no splashing or puddles."

"'Kay, Dad."

Nate returned to the kitchen and paused when he spotted Lucie bent over in front of the open oven. *Nice ass.* He was too late to stop the idea from forming, but he forced his gaze away as he headed for the sink. He could notice, but he wouldn't do anything further. It had been a long time, though, since he'd had a woman so attractive so close. He washed his own hands, then cleared his throat as she straightened, carefully putting the golden-crusted bread onto the counter. "Which way to the silverware?"

She glanced over her shoulder, a half-smile curving her mouth. "Second drawer from the end there, thanks."

He went there to carry out his self-appointed task, then, after opening a couple cabinets, found bowls, too.

Hayden rushed into the room, wiping one hand on his jeans and leaving a wet streak. "Mm, hot bread. I couldn't reach the light, Daddy."

Nate set the bowls on the table with the spoons and a butter knife. "I'll get it. You pick a seat and climb up." He headed for the powder room to check on the condition his son had left it in. Not bad, only a small splotch of water on the sink. He dried it off and hit the light.

In the kitchen, he discovered Hayden on a pink booster seat. Lucie smiled. "The table's a bit high without it."

"Thanks." Nate noted the three bowls full of steaming soup on the table. "Did you work in a restaurant in a former life?" he teased, sitting down on the chair closest to Hayden.

She chuckled as she sat across from him. "In high school, so it almost was another lifetime ago." She winked at his son. "I was almost as young as Hayden."

The little boy giggled and picked up his spoon.

Nate made sure his son was okay with his soup and bread before he turned his attention to his own dinner, which smelled *really good.* His stomach rumbled, so he dug in. *Wow.* "This is amazing, Lucie," he said after his first spoon-ful. "Thanks for inviting us." He felt bad for accepting the invitation so grudgingly.

She smiled again, then dropped her gaze to her spoon.

Hayden chattered in between bites of bread and soup, keeping them both involved in conversation for the duration of the meal. Lucie chatted easily with Hayden, but Nate noticed she didn't really offer up anything personal. He wondered why that bothered him.

On the other hand, he realized he hadn't shared anything either. Just casual conversation. Awkward.

"I'm full, Daddy," Hayden announced, his spoon clanking against his empty bowl. "That was yummy."

Lucie smiled again. "Thank you." She put her own spoon down, more quietly. "And thank you for coming. It was nice to have company for dinner."

His son giggled. "Thanks for askin' us."

Nate bit back a smile. At least his son's manners were good.

"You should have supper with us one night," Hayden continued.

Now he hid a wince. His cooking leaned more toward grills and microwavable meals, not homemade gourmet, like Lucie's.

She leaned her chin on one hand, looking at his son. "You cook, too?" she teased.

Hayden laughed. "'Course not, Daddy does."

"Ah." She smiled a little, and Nate noted the shadows in her eyes as she pushed to her feet. "Let me get your bowl, Hayden." She ruffled his son's hair before she picked up his empty bowl.

Nate noticed she hadn't agreed to dinner with them. He

rose, collecting his own bowl and his son's cup and followed her to the sink. "That was delicious," he reiterated. "You should join us one night. I can't promise it will be this good, though."

She smiled up at him. "Thanks. Here, let me get those." She took the dishes he held.

She still hadn't agreed to join them, just thanked him. He should be relieved. Instead, he was a little insulted. And more curious about her.

She turned back to them after a quick rinse of the bowls.

"Thank you, Lucie," Hayden said again, coming over to stand in front of her. "Will you play with me again?"

Her smile made Nate do a double-take. "I'd love to, when it's okay with your dad." She smoothed down the boy's hair.

His son grinned. "Yay!" He clapped his hands and gave a little hop.

"Why don't you get your jacket, buddy?" Nate waited until Hayden stepped over to the chair by the door. "Thanks again, Lucie. It was really nice of you to invite us."

She met his gaze with a half-smile. "It was nice to have company. It's been a while."

He wondered about that, since she'd only been here a couple of weeks, but while he was trying to decide if it was impolite to ask, his son rushed back to them.

"I'm ready, Daddy!"

He automatically fixed Hayden's jacket, with the hood bunched up inside the collar. "Well, then we should go, buddy." He caught a flash of sadness in Lucie's eyes when he looked at her again, but it vanished when her lips curved upward.

"Thanks, guys," she said, stuffing her hands into her sweater pockets.

"G'night!" Hayden rushed at her, wrapping his arms

around her legs before Nate or Lucie could stop him. "Thanks, Lucie!"

She swallowed, pulling her hands from her pockets to bend down and give him a hug. "You're very welcome, Hayden."

Definitely something there, Nate thought. He looked at her left hand—no ring, or any mark from a ring no longer worn, but that didn't mean she wasn't a parent, or step-parent.

Hayden released her and whirled around. "I'm ready, Daddy," he announced.

Nate nodded. "Then let's go." He met Lucie's shuttered gaze again. "We can talk about dinner another time."

"Sure." Her flat tone didn't make him think that would be a chat with a positive outcome, but he'd ask again anyway.

"Okay, buddy, let's go home. Think you can find the way?"

His son laughed. "'Course I can." He pushed the door open, and Nate followed, more slowly.

Lucie came to the door and waved to his son.

"Thanks again," he said, turning back once more.

Her smile was small but genuine. "It was nothing."

He wouldn't press any more tonight, so he stepped outside and followed his son across the yard. When he glanced back from the fence, the door was closed.

He sighed. It wasn't any of his business what might have happened in her past as long as it didn't affect them.

But he could still wonder.

Chapter Two

Lucie booted up her laptop in the morning while she waited for the tea kettle to boil. It was probably time to dust off and update her résumé, no matter what she'd said to Nate yesterday about her current location along the stages of grief. Eventually she'd have to give the house back to Harry and Mindi, whether she liked it or not.

She caught her lower lip in her teeth and looked at the sunshine through the window. It was too bad she couldn't stay here indefinitely. The island was a wonderful escape from the real world.

Sighing, she pushed to her feet. The kettle hummed as the water inside it neared a rolling boil. A nice cup of tea and maybe she could concentrate on the résumé for a little while. She turned the stove off just as the kettle began to whistle, then poured some of the hot water into her waiting mug, inhaling the fruity sweet aroma of the herbal tea and honey.

Then she carried it back to the table and squared her shoulders. Time to work.

It took several hours, but by the time she finished her second mug of now-cold tea, she thought she had a résumé she could work with. She pushed to her feet and stretched. Might need to let that sit for a while before looking at it with fresh eyes. She carried her mug to the sink and rinsed it, then parted the curtains to let more sunshine in.

That view... She smiled at the blue sky meeting the ocean in the distance. She could look at that every day. Though once she found a new job, it would almost certainly mean a view of walls and buildings instead of the shore.

She frowned, then caught some movement from the corner of her eye. She looked toward the lighthouse, where she could see a man walking in the room at the top of the tower. Nate.

Lucie wondered what he'd thought of dinner last night, really. He hadn't wanted to say yes to the invitation, but evidently couldn't say no to his son. She glanced up again, but he'd disappeared. Probably had work to do in his shop.

She shook her head. She needed to get outside and take a walk. Clear her head and breathe in some fresh sea air.

She glanced at the thermometer. Just a sweater, maybe. In two minutes, she was slipping her arms into the sleeves of her sweater on her way across the back yard, headed for the rocky path down to the shore.

She loved the walk on the beach, even though it wasn't a traditional sandy beach–sunbathers wouldn't come here, or, if they did, they'd quickly leave, disappointed. There was a narrow strip of coarse sand along the water's edge, peppered by large boulders, with a rocky field closer to the squatty cliff. Lucie paused for a moment on the wet sand, watching a pair of gulls squabble over a starfish. The winner, slightly bigger, flew away a moment later with his prize, to one of the big boulders near the water to beat it on the rock before gulping it down whole. The loser glided over to her, no doubt hoping for a hand-out, then flew off when she didn't produce anything.

She stuffed her hands into her sweater pockets and started walking again. She'd had more than enough time to brood, she thought. At least about losing her job. Before she'd fled her apartment in Portland, she'd already been holed up there for two weeks, when Mindi called to ask if she'd like a change of scenery.

Though to be honest, she'd been brooding even before the company was sold, and she knew it.

The break-up had happened a year ago, so she didn't even feel a twinge of pain about the abrupt and unexpected end of her relationship with Daniel. The lingering emotion had only to do with his son, Teddy, whom she'd loved. Lucie frowned. Daniel had been divorced for several years when she met him four years ago, and she'd been cautious—dating a single dad could be dicey, depending on the relationship he had with his ex. But Daniel had a cordial relationship with Teddy's mom, even though she lived halfway across the country and rarely saw Teddy. Until Daniel suddenly decided his son needed to be closer to his mother, Lucie had begun to imagine a real future.

There had been no discussion, no warning. Just a stilted conversation over dinner one night that left her shocked and sick. She hadn't been able to think clearly enough to wonder why he didn't mention the possibility of her joining them until days later. She hadn't even gotten to say good-bye to Teddy, because Daniel had already packed up and left Port-land to move his son to St. Louis. With his ex-wife.

She still didn't know how that had happened, but she did miss Teddy.

Like yesterday, when Hayden had lobbed that ball at her.

She smiled a little, hunching into her sweater when a

gusty breeze blew in. Too much thinking about the past for one morning. She stopped walking and turned around. She had things to do. She walked faster toward the trail up the cliff.

By the time she got back to the path, she'd discarded her sweater, tying it around her waist because she was so warm from her brisk walk. Halfway up the slope, she glanced up and saw Nate at the top of the lighthouse again. She waved before stopping to think about whether she should or not, but he waved back.

Now she didn't feel quite so dumb. She climbed the rest of the trail to the top, smiling. Until she reached the yard and heard a saw running and realized Nate couldn't be in the lighthouse and running equipment in his shop at the same time.

She stopped, looking up at the tower, where the man still stood. From here, she couldn't see his face. It must be his father.

She frowned, though, when she got closer to the house and saw only the usual big black truck in his driveway. Weird.

And none of her business, really.

She had work of her own to do. Kind-of. Wincing, she headed inside. There were job search websites waiting for her to join and browse. *Ugh.*

———

HAYDEN WAVED UP AT THE TOWER, AND NATE GLANCED OVER his shoulder to the hazy shape of Micah silhouetted against the window. "Come on, Hayden, Grandma's waiting for you."

"'Kay, Daddy, I'm comin'." His son ran a few steps to

him, and he scooped the boy up into his car seat. "Buckle me in!"

He smiled as he did so. "I heard a rumor there might be a surprise waiting for you today."

"A s'prise?" His son's eyes rounded. "What kinda s'prise?"

"If I told you, it wouldn't be a surprise, would it?" He ruffled his son's untidy hair. "You'll have to wait and see. Hands inside the ride." He shut the door and rounded the truck to his own seat. As he slid in, he caught a movement from the corner of his eye and looked over at Harry and Mindi'–Lucie stood at the sink, head down. He started the truck, and she lifted her face, looking first at the truck and then away–toward the lighthouse, where Micah still stood.

When she looked at him again, he saw her frown. He waved, smiling grimly and wondering if Lucie believed in ghosts.

"Bye, Lucie," Hayden shouted, waving wildly.

Even though she couldn't possibly hear him, she smiled and waved at Hayden as Nate backed the truck out of the driveway.

When he parked at his parents' a few minutes later, he was still wondering–not everyone could bring themselves to believe in things like ghosts. Harry and Mindi had lived on the island long enough to have gotten over that, but if Lucie didn't believe... Well, it didn't matter, because she wouldn't be here long. Just curious, he supposed, stopping the truck behind his father's. It was always an interesting conversation with newcomers, about the lighthouse ghost.

Growing up on the island, he'd known about Micah all his life. His ex had thought it was sad and romantic–until she left, just like Micah's lost wife had done, escaping the island with a new man and leaving Nate and Hayden behind.

He frowned, pushing open his door. It was better that she'd gone when she did–better for Hayden because he was so young.

"Gram!" Hayden shouted as Nate opened the passenger door.

Nate glanced over his shoulder and saw his mother waving from inside the house. "Let me get you unbuckled, buddy, and then you can go see her." He unclipped the harness and hefted his son out of the truck, giving him a little bounce just to hear him giggle, before setting the boy on his feet. He followed his son to the back door, noted his dad's silhouette in the open workshop door out back, then shifted his attention to his mother, who'd opened the screen door to let Hayden inside.

"Take your jacket off, Hayden," she called as he rushed past her. Her gaze landed on Nate. "I hear you met the house-sitter."

He blinked. "I don't think she's exactly house-sitting."

"Really?" One of his mother's eyebrows winged up. "What is she then?"

"Friends with Harry and Mindi." He shrugged.

"Hm." She glanced over her shoulder at a thump from the next room. "Hayden?"

"I'm good."

Nate repressed a smile. "I can get him in a few hours, maybe before he destroys the place."

Ida Baxter laughed. "Too late." She met his gaze again. "Is she pretty?"

Oh hell. He shrugged. "I guess."

His mother's eyes narrowed a tiny bit. "Hayden likes her."

"She played with him." He lifted one shoulder a little again. "She'll be gone soon."

"Hm."

He ignored the speculative look in her eyes. "I have a client appointment before I head back to the shop. I'll pick up the human wrecking ball by four-thirty. Thanks, Mom."

She sighed as he turned away. "We'll see you then."

Nate didn't look back–he'd learned a long time ago not to encourage his mother when she started wondering about his love life, or lack of one. And no matter how pretty Lucie was, he wasn't in the market for a relationship, and she wasn't staying on the island. Problem solved.

———

LUCIE LOOKED UP FROM HER LAPTOP AT THE SOUND OF A door closing nearby. Nate and Hayden, she thought, and went back to the job search on her screen. Then the next search, and the next. She got up from her seat at the dining room table, stretching, to turn on lights when the daylight waned. Her stomach rumbled a complaint. She'd been at this so long, she'd missed lunch. She had some soup left from last night, she mused as she stretched. That would have to do for tonight. Tomorrow, she could roast some vegetables to go with a piece of the fish she had in the fridge.

As she waited for the microwave, she noted the lighthouse light rotation, and the silhouette against the window. She glanced at the house next door, but the curtains were drawn.

She should have noticed by now if Nate had a helper over there, she thought as the microwave beeped. So who was the man in the lighthouse?

A trick of the light? She didn't think so. He'd waved at her that morning. She hadn't imagined that.

She took her bowl from the microwave and put a slice of

bread in next for a few seconds, just long enough so when she put butter on, it would melt into the bread.

There was someone in the lighthouse.

She looked up, watching the man pace back and forth inside the room at the top of the tower.

Nate must be aware, or he wouldn't have just driven away that morning with someone up there. She should quit worrying about it.

She sighed and put the thick, hot slice of bread on the edge of her bowl. It was none of her business.

That didn't stop her thinking about it while she sipped her soup and watched the local news. It was silly. Who cared if the neighbors had someone who worked in their lighthouse? She shook her head and pushed to her feet. If she wasn't careful, by the time she left the island, she'd be one of those nosy small-town busybodies people joked about who knew everyone else's business.

She tamped down a smile at that idea. There wasn't much danger of that since she'd only met a handful of islanders since her arrival, on her single trip to the small general store near the ferry dock right after she'd arrived. Besides that, the only people she'd met were Nate and Hayden. She carried her bowl to the kitchen to wash her few dirty dishes.

The task took just a few minutes, and while she worked, she steered her thoughts to the job searches she'd started that day. She'd thought she knew how she'd spend the rest of her professional life. Now, though...well, she wondered if now was the time to really take a chance, to figure out what made her happy and how to get there. She hadn't imagined herself in an office or a cubicle when she was a kid.

Lucie jumped at the knock on the back door, then used her elbow to shut off the faucet, grabbing the dish towel to dry her hands on the way to the door. She turned on the light over the door, and her eyebrows rose at the sight of Nate on the steps, Hayden hanging from his back. She tugged the door open. "Hi, guys."

"Hi, Lucie."

She frowned at the grim expression on Nate's face. "Are you okay?" She tossed the towel toward the counter.

"We're fine, but my dad isn't. The paramedic unit just landed the helicopter to take him to the mainland hospital. I hate to ask...to bother you, but I need to get my mom to the ferry to go to the hospital, and I wonder if you'd mind hanging out with Hayden for a while."

Startled, she blinked at him. "Sure."

"At our house?" He winced. "It'll be bedtime soon."

"Of course, let me grab my sweater. Come on in." She hurried away to the living room to shut off the TV and pick up her heavy sweater from the arm of the couch. She grabbed her phone and the book she'd left on the coffee table last night. She might need some entertainment after Hayden was in bed. When she turned around, Nate stood inside the closed door, stress framing his mouth and eyes with faint lines. "Let's go," she said, summoning a smile.

After making sure she had the key in her pocket, she locked the door and pulled it shut. She hurried after Nate, whose long strides got him to the fence several seconds before her. She followed him across the yard and into his house, pausing in the mud room to kick off her sneakers, before emerging into a kitchen that made her want to drool— gorgeous honey-toned cabinets with pale, gold-flecked stone counters, and a serious stove that actually made her stop mid-step to gawk at the six burners and built-in griddle. Shaking her head, she dragged her gaze away from it to where Nate crouched a few feet away, unzipping Hayden's jacket.

The little guy was in pajamas already, soft, fuzzy blue

covered with cartoon characters in bright colors. He turned away from his dad to grin up at her. "Hi, Lucie."

She smiled back. "Hiya." She met Nate's eyes, and her smile faded. "We'll be fine, Nate. What time is bedtime?"

"Eight." He swallowed, then stuck his hand into his pocket, and she heard the faint clink of his keys. "We usually read a story first, but just one. I don't know how long I'll be, Lucie. Are you sure–"

"I'm positive," she interrupted, stepping toward him to pat his arm. "We'll be fine. I have some kid experience, I promise." She stopped herself from hugging him. She didn't know him well enough for that, even though he looked a little shell-shocked. "You go get your mom. Maybe leave your cell number by the phone."

He nodded, then bent to kiss his son's head. "You be good, buddy."

"'Kay, Daddy."

After another few seconds' hesitation, he took a quick breath and squared his shoulders. "I really appreciate it, Lucie."

"No problem," she said lightly. "I'll see you later." She watched him scribble on a note pad near the kitchen phone, then lock the door behind himself on the way out. She turned to the little boy who stood a few feet away. "So, we have some time before you have to go to bed. What do you usually do before story-time?"

A sly smile curved his mouth. "We could have a snack."

She laughed and dropped to her knees in front of him. "Let me see your teeth."

His smile vanished. *Busted.* "How'd you know I already brushed?"

"I wasn't kidding when I said I had some kid experience,

buddy." She tweaked his chin, and he smiled again. "Do you want to play a game?"

He caught her hand and led her into the next room. The living room was tidy, though she noted the toy chest in one corner near the stairs. Daniel's living room had never been so neat. Teddy's toys were always scattered around.

Lucie tamped down the flare of pain at that memory. "Wow, did you already clean up for the night?"

"Yep. While Daddy made supper. The games are in the closet, but I can't reach 'em." He pointed to the sliding doors near the front door.

"Let's see what we've got." She crossed the braided rug between the sofa and coffee table to the closet and slid one door open. "Hm. Which one is your favorite?"

"The dominoes!"

She spotted the picture dominoes and stretched up to get the box from the top of the stack. "Do you want to play in the kitchen or in here?"

"Here. On the coffee table." Hayden took the box from her and ran back to the sofa. "You gotta match the pictures on the dominoes."

"I see that." Lucie dropped onto the floor in front of the leather couch and lifted the lid from the box. "Can you turn all of them over so the pictures are looking down?" She pushed a stack of thick history books to the far end of the table, out of the way.

Hayden set to work, and she took a quick look at the directions to make sure there wasn't anything else she needed to know.

"Okay, let me mix them up, and then you get to pick seven. Do you know how many that is?"

"Maybe." A frown wrinkled his forehead, and she bit back a smile.

"Okay, you take one, then I'll take one, and then you again, until we each have seven to start." She helped him when he lost count after five, and then let him go first.

After three games, Hayden looked at the big clock on the front wall. "It's almost story-time. We should clean up."

Lucie smiled. "You can tell time?"

He laughed. "No, but I know where the hands are on the clock for story-time. Daddy showed me."

"Okay, then let's clean up, and we can start story-time." She blinked in surprise when he hurriedly scooped up little handfuls of dominoes to put into the box. She held up one hand when he reached for more. "I have a faster way." She took the box from the other end of the table and held it just under the edge of the coffee table. "Now push." She winked at him.

He giggled, then shoved dominoes off the table and into the box. "I like this way better!"

"I bet you do." Lucie put the lid on the box and replaced it on the closet shelf. "Lead the way, buddy."

He caught her hand and pulled her toward the steps. Upstairs, he towed her into the first room on the right, and she flipped the light switch inside the door, illuminating a room with pale yellow walls, and several bright wall decals around the room. Hayden released her and rushed to the low bookcase on the opposite wall. She took a moment to study the fat teddy bear flying an old-fashioned red bi-plane on one wall, and the grinning dog with long flapping ears speeding in a blue car on another.

"This one, Lucie! Please." Hayden's book jabbed her in the thigh before he stretched his arm up.

She took the fat book and gave him a suspicious, squinty look over the top of it. "I don't think we can read this whole thing before bedtime, mister."

He laughed. "No, it's a whole buncha stories, but my favorites are in it."

"Ah, okay. Well, then you'd better climb in and get comfortable."

"Daddy sits in the chair and I sit on his lap." He pointed behind her.

"Got it." She took the few steps to the rocking chair in the corner and sat, feeling a little pang when he clambered up onto her knees. "All right, which story should we start with?"

He paged through the book until he reached a story with a picture of a boy in a treehouse at the top of the page. "This one."

Lucie smiled. "All right. Get comfy."

He snuggled into her lap, and she started to read. Even though it was one of his favorites and he must have heard it countless times, he giggled in all the right spots, adding excited comments as she read about the boy's exploits in his treehouse. The next story was an adventurous tale with a talking dog and his monkey friend hunting for a treasure. By the time she'd finished that one, Hayden's eyes drooped, but he flipped several more pages. "Last one," he said, cuddling closer.

She started to read, though she paused for a moment when she realized the boy in the story was searching for his mother. By the time she reached the end of the story, with the fictional boy happily settled with both his father and mother, Hayden slept, fully relaxed against her.

Carefully, Lucie set the book on the floor beside the chair and shifted the little boy so she could get to her feet. Another careful maneuver to tug down the blankets on his bed, and then she eased him into it, tucking the sheet, blankets and comforter up under his chin. He didn't bat an eyelash, soundly asleep. She brushed his blond hair away from his forehead and kissed his round cheek. "Sleep well, buddy," she breathed as she stood again. She put his book away, and then shut off the light, pulling the door most of the way closed. There was a night light in the hall, probably in case Hayden needed to get up during the night.

She returned to the main floor. Her book lay on the coffee table, and her sweater on the arm of the couch. She realized she was cooler now that Hayden wasn't snuggled up against her, so she put her sweater back on and wandered into the kitchen. The countertops were cool beneath her fingers, and she admired the cabinets. In the sunshine, the kitchen must be stunning. But the stove...well, she wanted to cook on a stove like that. Not that Harry and Mindi's stove was terrible. It wasn't, it was perfectly functional, but Lucie had always had delusions of grandeur in the kitchen. She liked to cook and to bake, and she'd always wished she had an amazing stove for both of those things.

Who was she kidding? As a kid, she'd wanted to have a restaurant and have an even bigger stove than Nate had.

She laughed at herself. Silly. She hadn't thought about that in years. Not since she went off to college and studied business and marketing courses–her parents had drilled the need for security into her head. It might have been more helpful if they'd also told her she might have to start over unexpectedly someday.

She swallowed and left the kitchen. She was an adult now, and she needed to be practical, not fanciful.

But for tonight, she decided to take a page from one of her favorite classic books and put that off until tomorrow. Tonight, she could read and pretend she didn't have adult problems.

Chapter Three

Nate breathed easier when he drove the truck onto the island from the ferry. Mort gave him a thumbs-up, so he waved, then steered toward home.

He hoped Hayden had behaved. It had been a long time since he'd entrusted his son to anyone besides his parents. He hoped Lucie was really up to the task.

When he got to the house, the porch lights were still on, but he couldn't see more than faint light around the curtains downstairs. He climbed out of the truck, exhausted. He couldn't even summon the energy to square his shoulders for whatever he might find inside.

The house was quiet. Completely silent. He shut the door softly behind him, toeing off his sneakers and shrugging out of his jacket before he headed into the kitchen. The supper dishes stood in the drainer. He frowned, then continued to the living room. Where he found Lucie sound asleep on the sofa. The ugly orange and brown afghan he kept draped across the back of the sofa was tucked up around her shoulders, and a lock of her dark hair had slid forward, over her cheek.

He hesitated, hating to disturb her sleep. He glanced at the clock. Almost two. Fuck, it was later than he'd realized. No wonder he was so tired. He rubbed one hand down over his face and took a slow breath. He'd just let her know he was home, and she should stay where she was. He bent over and touched her shoulder.

Lucie jerked awake, sitting up so fast she almost knocked her head against his chin before he straightened.

"Whoa," he said softly, holding both hands out. "Easy, Lucie. Just me."

Her wide eyes squeezed shut for a moment, and she let out a quick breath. "Sorry. You startled me."

"It's okay. I just wanted you to know I was home. Lie down, go back to sleep, it's late."

She met his gaze, her sleepy green eyes searching. "How is your dad?"

Tension squeezed his chest again. "He was in recovery when I left. The doctor pinned the bones in his leg back together." He sat down on the coffee table.

Lucie surprised him by reaching over to pat his knee. "You must be very worried. I'm sorry."

He caught her hand. "Lie down, Lucie. Or I can make up the bed in the guest room."

"I can go back over to Harry and Mindi's," she said, covering a yawn with her free hand. "You should get some sleep. I imagine you're exhausted."

"You, too. Thanks for staying with Hayden. Did he give you any trouble?"

"Of course not. We played some picture dominoes, then read a couple stories, and he was out."

"You didn't have to wash the dishes."

A faint smile touched her mouth. "I needed something to do. And I love your kitchen. You did that?"

Nate nodded and gave her fingers a gentle squeeze. "Go back to sleep, Lucie. Really."

She shook her head, yawning again. "I don't want to be in your way, and I have a bed just a few yards away." She smiled once more.

He realized he was still holding her hand and released it, standing. "You aren't in the way. I really appreciate your help."

She eased to her feet, too. "If you need a hand again, let me know."

"Do you have kids?"

Her smile faded. "No, no kids."

"But you're good with him."

Her mouth turned down a little. "I dated someone for a few years who had a son a bit older than Hayden."

"I'm sorry, it's none of my business."

She shook her head. "Old news. But I do miss Teddy sometimes." Her smile this time was forced. "Let me get my shoes and sweater on, and I'll get out of your way so you can sleep, too."

Nate closed his mouth on a curse. He hadn't meant to make her feel bad. "Lucie."

She glanced back over her shoulder.

He didn't even know what he'd meant to say, and it didn't matter when a loud rumble of thunder shook the house.

Her eyes widened, and she looked toward the back door as a bolt of lightning flashed over the sky. Right before the rain started, pouring down in a deluge. "Shit," she whispered, her shoulders slumping.

"Come on," he said. "I'll make the bed upstairs in the guest room."

"It's fine. I can make it across the yard."

"You'll be soaked before you get to the gate, Lucie."

She turned around slowly. "I hate to—"

He sighed.

She flushed. "I can sleep on the sofa. It's very comfortable. And then I can get out of your hair before Hayden realizes I'm still here."

Nate hadn't even thought about that. "He'd be thrilled." He smiled. "Let me at least get you a better blanket." He headed for the closet and pulled out a pillow and two blankets from the built-in chest. "Here." He put the pillow at the end of the couch where she'd had her head on her arm. "Come on, Lucie."

She hesitated another second or two before retracing her slow steps to the sofa.

"Lie down."

A little line appeared between her eyebrows.

He waited.

Finally, she dropped onto the sofa again and he spread the first blanket over her, then the second. Her solemn green eyes stayed on his face the entire time, and he wondered what she was thinking. Without thinking, he stroked her hair away from her face. "Relax. Go back to sleep."

She closed her eyes, then exhaled roughly before rolling onto her side.

"There you go." He turned off the light on the end table, leaving the room mostly dark. Light from the kitchen illuminated the other end of the room, and a night light came on near the stairs. "Sleep well." He returned to the kitchen and turned off the light over the sink, finding his way to the steps without trouble.

Upstairs, he checked in on Hayden, who had one arm flung over his head, and the blankets tangled around his waist. Smiling, Nate adjusted the covers and brushed a kiss on his son's head before he went to his own room across the hall. He sank onto the edge of his bed in the dark and took a few slow, deep breaths. He could still hear the panic in his mother's voice when she'd called earlier–it had made his heart hammer in his chest and in his ears. His mother was unflappable. Always. Until tonight, when his father had fallen off the tall ladder at the side of the house.

Nate let out a hard breath and stretched out on the bed, one arm over his face. She'd scared him, probably as much as his father had scared her.

At least Lucie had been willing to come over. He didn't know what he'd have done if he'd had to take Hayden to the hospital with him.

He wondered about the ex-boyfriend with the little boy. She didn't seem bothered about the ex, just sad about his son. For the best, he supposed. Better to get it out of the way early. Like his own.

Shit.

He shoved upright again and stripped off his shirt and jeans, then went into the connecting bathroom to wash his face and brush his teeth. Then he climbed into bed and tried to think of nothing but the sound of the thunder and lightning over the pounding rain on the roof.

His mother had stayed at the hospital in spite of the doctor's assurance that his father would spend the next few hours sleeping off the anesthesia. She wouldn't be budged. He'd need to take her some things when he went back.

His eyes opened again. He couldn't take Hayden to the hospital.

Maybe...

He didn't want to take advantage of Lucie either.

He watched a bright flash streak across the sky with the next lightning strike. He didn't have to figure out tomorrow tonight. Even though it was really tomorrow already.

He groaned and yanked the blanket over his head. He needed sleep so he could think clearly in the morning.

———

WHEN HE WENT DOWNSTAIRS A FEW HOURS LATER, LUCIE WAS gone. The blankets were folded neatly and stacked on the pillow at the end of the sofa, the afghan draped along the back in its usual place. He shoved one hand through his wet hair and glanced toward the window, but the curtain was still closed. He wondered if she'd slept at all. The sofa was comfortable, but after he'd woken her and the storm started, she might've had trouble going back to sleep.

He padded into the kitchen and poured a glass of orange juice, then stood at the sink to drink it, looking out at the grey morning, the incoming whitecaps. His mother hadn't called, so nothing else had happened. That was good.

He jotted down a few things to pick up for her, then paused when he heard light footsteps behind him. "Hey, buddy, you're up early."

"I was lookin' for Lucie." Hayden rubbed his eyes, disappointment curving his mouth down. "I thought she'd be here."

"She went home to her own bed." Nate set his glass on the counter and scooped his son up. "Did you have fun last night?"

"Yes! We played dominoes, and I beat Lucie. And she read my favorite stories."

Nate hid a wince. "That's good. Were you on your best behavior?"

His son tsked. "I was a good boy."

He smiled and ruffled the little boy's messy hair. "Glad to hear it. How about we get you some breakfast, so you can get dressed? I have to get some things for grandma, and...” He stopped. He'd have to think about that.

By the time Hayden was fed and dressed, Nate had run out of ideas. If he took his son to the hospital, he'd be bored in no time. He didn't have a lot of options here.

The tap at the back door startled him, and he leaned around the doorway to the mudroom to find Lucie waiting outside. He frowned. She couldn't have slept much if she was here already, dressed and freshly showered.

He pulled the door open. “Hi.”

“Hey.” She smiled. “I thought maybe you'd need a hand with Hayden if you're going back to the hospital. Is there any news?”

He shook his head. “Come in.” She'd come back. “I didn't want to impose on you again, so I was thinking about taking him with me.”

She chuckled. “How long do you think he'll last?”

She had a point. “Yeah, I thought about that,” he admitted.

“Look, Nate. I can only look at job search sites for so long before I lose my mind, and you need to see your dad, probably check on your mom. I can stay with Hayden. Or he can come over with me. I don't mind. Really.”

Nate squelched the relief bubbling up in his gut. “It would be a huge help,” he said after a moment.

She smiled. “Then we're set. Are you heading out soon?”

“I have to swing by my parents' to pick up a few things–” he glanced at the clock on the microwave– “and if I go now, I can catch the next ferry.”

“Then you should go. We're good.”

“You can call if you need me.”

“Okay.” She unbuttoned the top button on the heavy green sweater she wore.

"Lucie!" Hayden ran into the kitchen, grinning. "I thought I heard you."

"Good ears, kiddo." She ruffled his messy hair. "I'm going to hang out with you today, okay?"

"Yaaay!" His son jumped up and down several times while he shouted.

Nate relaxed. "You're going to be a good boy while I'm gone, right?"

"Always, always, always!" He jumped with each shouted word.

Lucie chuckled. "I'll try to keep the house in one piece for you." She winked, and he felt a flicker of _want_ as she turned to his son.

He squelched that, too. Not appropriate. Though he knew it was a bad idea, he couldn't stop his gaze from meandering down to the curve of her hips in faded jeans. _Stop it._ He dragged his gaze back to his son, who held up a small figure for her inspection. "Don't forget naptime, buddy."

Hayden frowned at him. "I'm gettin' to be a big boy. Big boys don't nap."

"Oh, but I nap," Lucie said before Nate could argue. "Even my dad takes naps." She smoothed Hayden's hair. "We'll give it a try later."

Nate relaxed. She'd do just fine. "I'll call to check in. Come here, buddy." He caught Hayden and smiled when his son squeezed him hard around the neck and pecked a kiss on his cheek. "I'll see you later." He met Lucie's gaze. "Thank you."

She smiled and shrugged "No problem. We're fine. Go."

He went. In under fifteen minutes, he'd collected the things for his mother and was on his way to the ferry.

But when he got to his father's room, it was empty.

Frowning, he retraced his steps to the nurses' station. "Excuse me, can you tell me where my dad is? Max Baxter."

The older woman behind the desk looked up from the papers she'd been studying. "Mr. Baxter had surgery this morning. Your mom is downstairs in the surgical waiting room on the second floor. She wanted me to tell you not to worry, it's just a minor procedure."

Nate's heartbeat quickened. "How can I find her?"

The nurse gave him directions, and he headed back to the elevator. Another surgery? Two floors down, he found his mom pacing around a seating bank at the far end of the hall, and he strode toward her.

Her smile was strained when she faced him. "Hi, Nate." She gave him a tight hug.

He hugged her back. "Are you okay?"

"Just tired. Dad's fine. The doctor didn't like the x-ray this morning, so he went back in to place a new pin to make sure things stay put, that's all. Dad's in recovery right now. They said he'll be ready to move back to his room shortly."

Nate forced some tension from his shoulders, taking and releasing a slow breath. "Is this a temporary pin?"

"Permanent. Dad'll set off all the metal detectors from now on." Her smile widened. "He'll hate that."

He chuckled. "Yeah, he will. Why don't you sit down?"

"I've been sitting too long, I need to move. Where's Hayden?"

"At home. Lucie offered to stay with him."

His mother shot him a sharp glance. "Really?"

He tamped down the urge to wince. "Yes. He likes her, and I trust her. And can you imagine him here for longer than ten minutes?"

Ida laughed this time. "Oh God, no. But maybe you should bring him by at some point. Your dad could probably use some cheer from his boy." She sighed. "He's going to hate being immobile, you know."

"I know." He did. He'd hate it, too. "You know I can help out."

"Thanks. I'll probably need a hand."

It occurred to him then that he couldn't take Hayden to his parents' while he worked, at least not for a while. He'd have to figure that out later. Right now, his attention shifted to the man in blue scrubs emerging from the double swinging doors at the other end of the room.

"Mrs. Baxter." The man crossed to them and offered his right hand to Nate. "You must be Max's son. I'm Dr. Wayne. We're going to take Max upstairs in about thirty minutes. He's awake, and we're adjusting pain meds, and then he'll be ready to escape recovery."

"This additional pin," Nate started. "Is this the last surgery?"

The older man nodded. "Barring anything unforeseen, yes. Now we just keep an eye on the break and make sure nothing shifts. Keep him from putting any weight on the leg, or using it at all."

His mother laughed. "That will be a challenge."

He winced, silently agreeing. His father was pretty active. Forcing him to do the exact opposite *would* be a challenge, one they would fail if Hayden was there every day. *Shit.*

Ida sighed as the doctor retreated to the recovery area. "I guess the good news is our bedroom is on the first floor."

Nate followed her to one of the sofas, dropping down onto the cushion beside her. "Yeah. If he has to stay off the leg, that probably means a wheelchair, doesn't it?"

"Sounds that way. He's really going to hate that." She covered her eyes with one hand and chuckled again. "World's worst patient, times ten."

"I'll get a ramp up before he comes home."

"That will help." She patted his knee. "I'm going to have my hands full, Nate."

"I know. We'll be fine." He tried not to think about the kitchen he was supposed to deliver next week–he still had all the staining to do on it. He reined that in. He'd do it. He'd managed to do his job and care for his infant son when Greta had left them, surely he could manage for a few weeks now with less help from his parents.

LUCIE SHOULD'VE KNOWN NAP-TIME WOULD BE AN ISSUE.

Hayden frowned at her from the foot of the steps, hands fisted at his hips. "I'm not tired."

She tamped down a smile at that bald-faced lie. "I promised your dad we'd do nap-time, and I don't break promises, buddy."

The little boy's expression shifted to something different, more cunning. "You said you take naps."

She smiled this time. "I do."

"Then you gotta take one, too. Wif me."

Gotcha. "Well, first I have to clean up our lunch mess."

His frown returned. "You hafta nap, too."

"Are you going to help me clean up in the kitchen?"

"'Kay." He trotted toward her again, startling her.

He was good. She restrained a sigh and followed him into the kitchen. The clean-up wouldn't take long really. She might actually have to take a nap, or at least lie down with him. Wouldn't be the first time–just the first time in a couple of years–she'd been outsmarted by a pre-schooler.

Hayden actually did try to help, putting his plate and cup in the dishwasher, and his napkin in the trash, plus a bunch of crumbs on the floor. Lucie ruffled his hair. "Thanks, buddy. Now it's time."

He didn't argue, just led the way upstairs, but he came to a stop in the doorway to his room. "I don't think you'll fit in my bed, Lucie."

"I don't either, buddy. But I can sleep on the sofa."

He narrowed his blue eyes. "But then I can't see if you're nappin'. You hafta nap up here. I'll get you one of Daddy's pillows." He ran across the hall before she could stop him, then reappeared, dragging a pillow with him. "Here. You can sleep beside my bed." He swung the pillow toward her.

Lucie caught it. "Okay." There was no point arguing. If she lay down next to his bed until he fell asleep, no big deal.

Hayden climbed up onto his bed and wrestled the blankets for a moment until he could slide between them. "Right there," he said, pointing at the floor beside his bed.

She put the pillow down, then tucked his blankets around him. "Okay. Close your eyes."

"When you do."

She smiled. "All right." She lowered herself to the floor, winking when he leaned over to watch, then stretched out. "All right, I'm going to close my eyes. One, two, three." She shut her eyes, listening to him flop down and sigh. "Are your eyes closed?"

"Yep. Have a good nap, Lucie."

"You, too, Hayden."

For a few minutes, she listened to him fidget. Then it got quiet. She smiled again.

"Lucie?"

She winced. "Yeah, buddy?" She kept her tone low.

"I'm glad you moved here. Micah is too." He sounded drowsy.

"Who's Micah?" She should've let that go instead of keeping him talking.

"The lightkeeper."

"Oh." That explained that. "Okay, sleepy time," she whispered.

"'Kay," he whispered back.

This time when it got quiet, it stayed that way. She relaxed, listening to his even breathing. She needed to finish lunch clean-up. And maybe think about supper. She wondered what was in Nate's fridge and freezer. Maybe after nap-time, she'd take Hayden over to raid her fridge–she probably had something in it that would need to be used up soon. She couldn't remember right now what she'd picked up at the store.

She jerked awake, then blinked up at the small face hovering above her.

"You really took a nap."

Lucie took a slow breath. "I told you I take naps." She just hadn't meant to do it today.

Hayden smiled, still hanging over the side of the bed. "I din't believe you took naps."

She reached up to tweak his nose, making him giggle. "Now you know I don't lie." She pushed upright. "Okay, buddy. Time to think about what you're having for supper." As she got to her feet, he scrambled out of bed.

"It's not suppertime yet." He caught her hand.

"I know, but if I figure it out now, you'll be able to eat on time." She bent to scoop up the pillow from the floor. "Can you put this back for me? I want to wash my hands."

"'Kay." He took the pillow and hurried across the hall while she went into the bathroom next door.

Her shoulder-length hair was a mess from her unplanned nap, so she did her best to finger-comb it into order again, then headed downstairs with Hayden, who plopped onto the sofa with a book while she continued into the kitchen.

No meat in the fridge, she discovered, so she opened the freezer. Plenty there, but now that she stood in front of Nate's food, she remembered the chicken in her fridge. No defrosting necessary. Plus veggies in the crisper. She could roast them all together and have dinner in one pan. Less clean-up later.

"Hey, buddy!" She turned away from the fridge and came up short when she found Hayden a foot away, a book in one hand. "Oh, there you are. We need to run over to my place to get some things for supper. Let's get your jacket."

"What're we havin'?" He followed her into the mud room and dropped his book on the bench inside the door.

"I'm going to roast a chicken and some veggies to go with it. Are you a good baker?" She helped him into the jacket, then tugged her sweater on.

"I help Grandma bake cookies."

She made sure the back door was unlocked before she shut it behind them. "Well, that's excellent. I was thinking maybe we could bake a cake for dessert."

"I like cake."

She laughed. "I bet you do. Come on, let's do this."

In under ten minutes, they were back at Nate's. Hayden pulled up a step stool to the sink, and she let him 'scrub' potatoes and carrots with the vegetable brush while she prepped the chicken.

"What can I do next?" he asked when she handed him a towel and took over the veggies.

"Hm, let me think about that. After your fingers are dry, why don't you get your book from the mud room until I get this into the oven? It'll only be a couple minutes, and then we can mix up the cake."

"Okay!" He swiped at his hands with the dish towel, then threw it at the counter before he ran to the next room.

Shaking her head, Lucie quickly finished cleaning the potatoes and carrots, then added them to the roasting pan, sprinkled some salt and pepper over everything and drizzled a little oil before she covered it and put it into the oven. When she turned around, Hayden was seated at the table, but instead of looking at his book, he watched her. She smiled. "Do you like icing on your cake?"

"Oh, yeah!" He nodded solemnly. "Chocolate is the best."

"You think so?" She congratulated herself for thinking to grab the cocoa powder while they'd been at the other house. "Well, we might be able to do something about that." She winked at him when his eyes rounded.

He helped with the cake, too, dumping cupfuls of ingredients into the bowl for her, though she had to admit it wasn't as big a mess as it could have been. Teddy had been a much messier kitchen assistant. Lucie slid the cake pan into the second oven less than fifteen minutes later.

"Okay, now we mix up some icing, and clean up our mess, and we can actually read some of that book before the cake is ready to come out. What do you say?"

Hayden rushed at her and wrapped his arms around her legs. "Thank you, Lucie!"

She bent and gave him a hug. "You're welcome." Her chest squeezed a little, too, but she ignored it. "Thanks for being such a good helper. Okay," she said as she straightened, "let's make our icing, and then clean the table so we can read."

She needed more than a nap, she mused. She needed a good night's sleep to make up for last night. She was being too sentimental. A full night's sleep, and she'd be as good as new.

Chapter Four

Nate pulled the truck into his driveway in the last dusky light and shut off the engine. Light shone around the edges of the living room curtains, and further, from the mud room at the back of the house. When he'd called earlier, Lucie assured him they were fine and he should take his time, while Hayden giggled in the background. He sighed and pushed the door open. Stars sparkled already in the sky, and chilly air washed up over the bluff.

He strode to the back door, and, along with warmth, some delicious aromas rushed out when he opened it. He shrugged off his jacket, listening, but he didn't hear anything. After abandoning his sneakers, he stepped into the kitchen. The oven was on warm, so supper was in progress, and a cake covered in chocolate icing sat on a blue plate in the middle of the table. He raised an eyebrow, then heard light running footsteps upstairs, and he smiled.

"Daddy!"

By the time he reached the foot of the stairs, Hayden leaped from several steps up.

Nate caught him, enjoying the tight hug his son bestowed on him. "Hey, buddy."

"Supper's ready, Daddy! I helped."

"Did you?" He looked up and saw Lucie descending the stairs, a smile tugging at her mouth. "Lucie."

"You're just in time to eat." She stopped a few steps away.

"It smells amazing. You didn't have to go to so much trouble." He hefted his son to one arm as he moved backward to let her come down the last couple of steps.

"It wasn't any trouble. I like to cook, and this boy worked up quite an appetite." She winked at Hayden. "Let me get the pan out of the oven."

"We'll set the table." He followed her into the kitchen, bemused.

She moved the cake to the counter beside the sink, then took a roasting pan from the top oven. When she uncovered it, his mouth actually watered. Chicken and vegetables, roasted golden. The scent that had greeted him earlier magnified.

"I washed the veggies, Daddy."

He noted Lucie's quick grin at that. "I bet you did a good job. Can you get silverware while I get the plates?" He set Hayden down, with a pat on the behind to put him in motion.

Lucie carved up the chicken. "I bet you want a leg, don't you, Hayden?"

"I do!" His son managed to collect enough forks for the three of them, then hurried back to the table to put them down. "How'd you know?"

"Just a hunch," she said, taking a big serving spoon from the spoon rest beside the range. "How about you, Nate?"

"I guess I'd better have some white meat, so the other leg is left for the noisy one." He held out a plate. "Probably should feed him first." He tamped down the rush of warmth in his chest when she smiled at him.

"I think so, too." She dished up some vegetables and one of the drumsticks. "I'll take the other plates."

Nate didn't argue, just took his son's meal to the table and settled him on his booster seat. "You wait for us, buddy."

Hayden frowned, but didn't argue.

By the time Nate turned around, Lucie had two filled plates in her hands. "Thank you." He pulled out a chair for her, then took the plate she held out.

Hayden chatted around bites from his chicken leg, and Nate let him. Now that he'd sat down, exhaustion tugged at him. He ate and listened to his son, answered when he needed to. Lucie made easy conversation with Hayden, so he felt better about being gone all day.

"This is really good, Lucie," he said when Hayden had a mouthful of potato. "I appreciate this so much. You're a great cook."

She smiled, looking at her plate for a second. "I like to cook. For five minutes in high school, I thought I'd have a restaurant when I grew up." She met his gaze. "But I was a good daughter and headed off to college instead of the culinary institute."

He heard the note of regret in her tone. "Did you add that to your list of potential jobs for your search?"

Her eyes widened, and her smile faded. "I...no, I didn't."

"Why not?"

She looked at him blankly for a moment. "It didn't occur to me," she said finally.

"You should do it." He stabbed a carrot with his fork. "You're a great cook."

She frowned as she picked up her water glass. "Maybe." Her doubtful tone made him smile.

"You should do it, Lucie," Hayden chimed in. "The restaurant closed an' now we don't have anywhere to go out to eat."

She shifted her gaze from his son to him. "What?"

Nate rested his fork on the edge of his plate. "There was a family restaurant here on the island until about two months ago. The owner had a heart attack, so he can't manage it anymore, and his wife didn't want to do it alone, so they closed it. That's a really good idea, Hayden."

Lucie looked perplexed, a faint frown line between her eyebrows, her fork held loosely.

When Hayden scrunched up his face, Nate winked at him, prompting a grin. "Can I have more 'tatoes, Daddy?"

"Sure. Let me have your plate, buddy." He noted Lucie's little head-shake as he rose from his seat. She smiled at his son again, and he noted the affection in her eyes.

Lucie laughed in all the right places as Hayden chattered around bites of his meal, and Nate realized he was staring.

She was pretty. Her green eyes crinkled at the corners as she smiled across the table, briefly. His gaze slid to her mouth for a moment. Tempting.

He jerked his attention back to his meal. He had no time for tempting. Or for anything, really. There was enough on his plate—his son, his cabinet-making business. And now he'd spend more time running back and forth to his parents' once his dad got sprung from the hospital, until Max was mobile.

His gaze landed on her again, in spite of his best intentions, and she met it, her smile softening.

Fuck him.

Her eyes widened, darkening, and her smile faded. Awareness shifted her expression, and she dropped her gaze to her plate.

At least one of them had enough sense to know that would be stupid.

He took a quick drink from his glass and stuffed a piece of chicken into his mouth.

"Daddy, is Grandpa comin' home soon?"

Saved by his son. "Maybe in a couple days," he said after he swallowed his food. "But he broke his leg when he fell off the ladder, remember? So he's going to be in a wheelchair for a few weeks."

His son bit off a big chunk of meat from his chicken leg. "Does it hurt?"

"Yes, it does."

"Maybe he wants my bunny."

Nate smiled at that. "Maybe. I can ask him tomorrow."

"Does that mean I get to play with Lucie again?"

He winced at his son's excited tone.

"It sounds like it," she said, not sounding unhappy.

He glanced over at her, noting her genuine smile at Hayden. "Lucie," he started.

She looked over at him and raised one eyebrow, eloquently daring him to offer another option.

He didn't have one, so he cleared his throat. "Thank you."

Her smile reappeared, and Hayden cheered.

He should be grateful he had someone to help instead of trying to find ways to discourage her from assisting. Just because he was attracted to her didn't mean he had no self-control.

Of course he did. And he would damn well exercise it.

———

LUCIE DIDN'T ARGUE WHEN NATE REFUSED HER HELP WITH

the dishes. Her insides still quivered from the realization that he was attracted to her.

"I'll see you in the mornin', Lucie!" Hayden shouted, hopping on one foot.

She smiled as she put her sweater on. "Yes, you will." They'd already decided Hayden would join her after breakfast so Nate could cram in a few hours of work before he headed to the hospital to see his dad–and try to get his mother to come home rather than sleep on the less-than-ideal pull-out chair-bed in his dad's hospital room again.

She wasn't sure that was a battle he would win, but she understood his concern.

Hayden gave her a quick hug and then ran back to his book in the living room.

"I really do appreciate this, Lucie," Nate said from where he stood at the sink.

"It's nothing, Nate," she said lightly. "Keeps me from having to spend endless hours on job search sites and getting more depressed than I already am." She kept her head down as she buttoned her sweater up to her chin.

"It isn't nothing to me."

His firm, quiet tone snared her attention, and her mouth went dry. The shadows in his brown eyes made her curl her fingers around the edges of her sweater to keep from reaching out.

"I'm not accustomed to asking for help." He cleared his throat. "I appreciate it."

She swallowed. "It's no problem," she whispered. Dammit–hot, attracted to her, and vulnerable. Shit, that was trouble. She took a slow breath. "I'll see you in the morning then." She inched toward the door.

A hint of awareness darkened his eyes, but he stayed where he was. "Good night, Lucie."

She took two more steps, clearing the doorway to the mud room, and a little relief sank into her belly. Until she heard footsteps behind her.

Within reach of the back door, she whirled. He stood at the open doorway of the kitchen, undisguised desire in his eyes this time. Her heart skipped a beat, and she felt a quick rush of excitement that she tried to squash as he stepped into the mud room. She held her breath as he took another step. One more. Until he stood a foot away, and her breath rushed out.

He studied her face for a long moment, and she wondered what he saw, what he was looking for. Impulsively, she moved closer to him, noting the way his eyes rounded, and she stretched up to brush a kiss on his mouth, lingered for a second, then stepped back.

"Good night, Nate," she whispered, reaching behind her for the doorknob.

His dark gaze followed her out the door, and she turned away, a smile curving her lips.

Well. That was nice. She could deal with the repercussions another day, and, for now, be reminded she was still alive.

————

At least, that had been the plan. But she'd spent half the night staring up at the darkness and worrying. What if she'd imagined the interest? What if she'd just made a huge mistake?

Lucie had been at the kitchen table with the teapot for two hours already, and was contemplating heating water for more tea when the knock sounded at the back door at eight. Her breath snagged. Time to face the music. She bundled her sweater tighter as she went to open the door.

"Hi, Lucie!" Hayden bounded into the room, dragging his teddy bear by one leg. "I had cereal for breakfast. What'd you eat?"

She smiled, turning to watch him even though she was aware of his father stepping inside behind them. "I didn't have breakfast, just tea."

The little boy frowned. "Grandma says breakfast is im...imp...important," he said carefully. "You shoulda had some of my cereal."

She stifled a chuckle. "Thanks, Hayden. I'll make up for it later."

The door closed, and her urge to laugh vanished as she glanced back.

She blushed. "Good morning."

Nate's somber gaze locked on hers. "Good morning. Are you sure you're ready for this?"

She nodded. "Of course. We'll be fine. I think we might bake cookies this morning. Or bread. Maybe both." She shut her mouth to keep from chattering on stupidly.

The corner of his mouth twitched. "I'll pop in when I finish staining these cabinets. You might be ready to get rid of him by then."

She blinked.

"And maybe we could talk about last night," he added in an undertone that made more heat rush to her face.

"Um..."

He grinned, and the dimple in his right cheek made her breath catch.

"Hey, Lucie!"

She jerked her attention from the man in front of her to

the small boy running at her from the living room. "Yes, Hayden?"

He put his hands on his hips. "What're we doin' today?"

"How do you feel about cookies?"

His big blue eyes widened. "We're makin' cookies?"

She nodded. "And maybe some bread, too."

"Yay!" He ran around her, pumping his fists in the air, and she laughed.

"Hey, buddy." Nate scooped up his son, tipping him over his shoulder so the little boy giggled. "You're going to be a good boy, right? And not make a mess in Harry and Mindi's house."

"Yep! Put me down, Daddy!"

He obliged, and Hayden resumed his circular run around them.

Nate stepped nearer. "Are you sure?"

"Positive. Go get some work done. You must be way behind."

"You have no idea." His mouth twisted slightly. "All right. I'll see you in a few hours then."

She nodded, pretending that the heat of his arm so close to hers didn't affect her.

"Bye, Daddy!" Hayden paused to high-five his father, then jogged into the living room for his bear.

Nate met her gaze once more.

"We're going to have fun. Go to work," she said lightly, making a shooing motion with one hand.

He smiled slowly. "Are you kicking me out?"

She flushed again. "Yes. Go to work."

Something dangerous flashed through his eyes, almost too quickly for her to recognize it, but then he nodded. "I'll see you in a few hours."

She watched him turn and leave, her gaze sliding down

from his broad shoulders to his butt, covered in faded, slim-fitting denim. When she realized what she was doing, she forced her eyes up, in time for the door to swing shut. Lucie took a slow breath and turned to Hayden. She smiled. "So I was thinking about giant chocolate chip cookies."

"Yay!" He cheered again. "How giant? Big as my head?"

She swallowed down a chuckle. "That's probably too big for a cookie. Only a real giant could eat a cookie that big."

He squinted up at her. "There's no such thing as giants."

She winked. "That we know of. Come on, let's get started on these cookies, buddy."

He did pretty well, she mused later, when she slid the bread pans into the oven, not too much mess in the kitchen. He sat at the table, watching her when she straightened. "How about some lunch?"

His gaze slid to the cookies on the counter.

"You can have a cookie after," she said. "Do you like grilled cheese sandwiches?"

He nodded quickly several times.

"All right. You want to help with these, too? You've done a great job with the cookies and the bread."

He grinned. "Punchin' the dough was the best."

She chuckled. "It is fun. Very therapeutic some days." She tugged open the fridge to get out the butter and cheese. "How are you at buttering bread?"

The little boy's eyes narrowed. "Daddy doesn' let me use knifes."

"Ah. Well, I'll help, how's that?" She pulled the bread box open and snagged the bag there, then a plate from the cupboard on her way back to the table.

"'Kay." He stood on his chair again, watching her spread out the things she'd brought. "You need a knife."

"Yes, we do. Be careful there, buddy." She stepped away

just long enough to get a butter knife. "Okay, let's teach you how to put these together."

He giggled when he smeared a giant glob of butter onto the first piece of bread. "Like that?"

"Well, it's a good start, but we have to spread it out. Like this." She guided his hand, spreading the butter across the whole slice of bread. "See? This way, the bread will get nice and toasty when we put it in the pan."

He nodded. "I wanna try the next one."

"All right." She winced when he stabbed the knife down into the container, then came up with an even bigger blob than the first one.

"Like this?" He did spread it a little this time, though with so much on the knife, he still left large bits in his wake, and then poked the knife through the bread. "Oops." He looked over his shoulder at her, chagrined.

"It's okay. Can I help again?"

Hayden nodded.

She steered his hand, leaving a thinner coating of butter, then putting the remainder on a new piece of bread. "We just need enough to keep the bread from sticking to the pan. Like this." They buttered the rest of the third slice. "You want to try the last one?"

"Yep." He was much more careful this time, only scooping up a little onto the knife, then smearing it across half of the bread. "I din't break it this time!"

"No, you didn't. Good job. Just a bit more...Yes, just like that." She smiled when he grinned up at her. "Perfect. Now we'll put them together and I'll fry them up."

He licked his finger. "'Kay."

They put the cheese into the middle of the sandwiches, and Hayden giggled when he got more butter on his fingers. Lucie cleaned him off and put their sandwiches into the pan she'd prepped on the stove, just as a knock sounded at the back door.

"Daddy!" Hayden rushed to the door.

She smiled at his exuberance when he tugged it open.

"Hey, buddy." Nate stepped inside. "Smells good in here."

"It's lunchtime. We're havin' grilled cheese." He wrapped one arm around his father's leg. "I helped."

Nate glanced around. "Really?"

She laughed. "He's not that messy."

His brown gaze snapped to her face, and one of his eyebrows shot up. "Are you sure you're talking about my son?"

Hayden giggled again.

"Are you hungry? I just put the sandwiches on." She rubbed one suddenly sweaty hand on her thigh. "I haven't put anything away yet."

"I can make it, Daddy!" Hayden raced back to the table and climbed up onto his chair.

"Careful, buddy." His father crossed to the table in a few long strides. "How about if I help you?"

"I can do it."

Lucie smiled at the stubborn tone and turned away to find her spatula. Behind her, she heard the low rumble of Nate's voice as he murmured to his son and the higher pitch of Hayden's voice as they put the sandwich together. Then she heard heavy footsteps, and she glanced up at Nate's approach. She slid the other two sandwiches over in the pan, and he dropped his in.

"Those are some big cookies," he said, holding her gaze.

"Giant," Hayden shouted. "We're havin' them after lunch!"

"That's right," she managed, feeling heat slide up her throat to her face. "Did you get a lot done?"

"Not enough." His mouth thinned.

"Hayden is fine here."

He frowned.

Lucie took a quick breath. "I know, you don't want to have to ask, and you don't. I'm offering." She made her lips curve.

He nodded. "Thank you."

"Daddy!"

He turned away, and she let out a slow breath, turning her gaze back to the pan on the stove. Time to turn the sandwiches. She concentrated on that, tuning out the chatter behind her. Until she turned off the burner a few minutes later and turned around to get plates.

Except Nate already had three of them in his extended hand.

"Thanks." She took them and deftly scooped sandwiches onto each one. "Hayden, do you like triangles or rectangles?"

"Triangles!" he shouted from the table.

Smiling, she sliced all three sandwiches diagonally and handed a plate to Nate. "For the noisy one," she said.

He shook his head as he turned back to the table, and Lucie followed with the other two plates. She sat, then realized she'd forgotten her water. "Do you want a drink, too, Nate?" She crossed to where her glass sat on the counter. "I've got juice, milk and water."

"Water's fine, thanks."

She returned to the table a moment later and set his glass down before she dropped onto her seat again. "How's your sandwich, big guy?"

"Yum!" Hayden mumbled around a mouthful of sandwich.

She heard Nate's soft laugh and glanced over to see his smile disappear behind half of his grilled cheese. Warmth spread from her face to her throat. She needed to stop that. Stop looking at him like she would be here long enough for...anything. Stop thinking about *really* kissing him...

She jerked her attention back to her lunch. *Enough.* She made small talk with Hayden and Nate, careful not to sustain eye contact with the latter for longer than a couple of seconds at a time. No point, she reminded herself. She was just his temporary neighbor and baby-sitter, and she'd been stupid to kiss him.

She kept up the casual chit-chat as he cleared the remains of lunch and wiped off his son's messy face and hands after the cookies they had for dessert.

"Lucie."

She glanced over from rehanging the dish towel, noting the faint tension lines fanning out from his brown eyes. "You should take as much time as you need," she said, breaking eye contact to glance at the stove. He'd even cleared away the skillet, dammit. "Hayden and I'll be fine this afternoon."

He blew out a hard breath, and she looked up in spite of her best intentions.

"Really. I know you need to get more work done and then go to the hospital. This gives me a great excuse not to look at more completely irrelevant results to my job-site searches." She smiled. "Go on." She ignored the way her heartbeat kicked into a slightly higher pace when he nodded, the hard line of his mouth softening.

"Hayden."

The little guy looked up from his bear.

Nate crooked a finger, and his son ran several steps to him. Nate squatted down and brushed messy blond hair back from the little boy's forehead. "You're going to be a good boy all afternoon, right? And take a nap."

"'Kay, Daddy." He patted his father's cheek. "Take my bunny to Grampa."

Lucie covered her smile with one hand as Nate tried to restrain his own.

He cleared his throat. "Maybe I can talk Grandma into coming home today." He rose as Hayden squeezed his bear around the neck and ran to the sofa. "I'll call you from the hospital if it looks like I'll be later than I'm hoping." He took a step toward her, and her heart jumped up to block her airway. Then he stopped, and she let out a slow breath, ignoring the crazy pulse-beat in her ears. "Thanks, Lucie."

She nodded, watching as he strode to the back door, out. And she took a deep breath.

"Lucie, what're we doin'?" Hayden shouted from the next room.

She smiled and headed for the living room. "I have a couple ideas."

———

Nate eased the truck off the ferry, waving at Mort Junior before he drove toward home. The sun had set hours ago, and he'd been unable to persuade his mother to leave the hospital, even though his father groused at her to go home. When he called an hour ago, Lucie'd already fed Hayden.

His son would be ready for bed soon. And he needed to figure out how to get his father home from the hospital in two days. It sure couldn't be in the truck. Probably not his mother's car either.

He sighed. That would be a problem for tomorrow. Along

with trying to finish staining the cabinets for the Wells' kitchen in his workshop.

He swung by his parents' to grab the mail on his way home. His house was dark, but Harry and Mindi's looked bright and welcoming when he pulled into his driveway. The front porch was lit, and softer light glimmered around the edges of the closed curtains. He slid from the truck, shifting his shoulders to try to release some tension. When he exhaled roughly, his breath clouded the air in front of his face. Probably freeze overnight.

As he strode to the front door and knocked, he made a mental note to get the wheelchair ramp up at his parents' tomorrow, too.

The red interior door swung open as he reached for the handle of the storm door, then he froze.

Lucie had Hayden in her arms, his sleepy son with his face tucked against her throat. She looked damn good.

Shit.

He collected himself and pulled the outer door open, stepping inside. "Hi."

She smiled as Hayden burrowed closer to her, patting his back gently. "Hey," she said softly.

Nate closed the door and stuck his hands in his jacket pockets. "Looks like someone is worn out."

"We had a busy afternoon, playing catch and racing in the backyard. He ought to sleep really well tonight."

He didn't want to risk touching her–because he <u>wanted</u> to touch her. He wanted to brush the wisp of dark hair away from her jaw. He wanted to lean in and kiss her, more than that quick brush of lips the other night. He was stupid. He'd been stupid about a woman once before, and that was all he'd allow himself. He squared his shoulders. "Hey, buddy," he said low, touching Hayden's cheek.

His son flung up one hand to swat him away, turning his face further into Lucie.

An apology in her eyes made him pause, then he dipped his chin once.

"Hayden," she whispered, "Daddy's home."

After a second, his son's eyes fluttered open, and he looked over for a moment, then closed his eyes.

"Where's his jacket?"

"On one of the kitchen chairs." She turned to lead the way, and Nate couldn't help it when his gaze dropped to her ass. *Dammit.*

He found the jacket and picked it up. "Hey, buddy," he said again, "let's get your jacket on so we can go home."

His son made an indistinct sound of protest.

Smiling, Lucie shifted the sleepy boy to slide the jacket on one arm, then turned him so Nate was able to get his other arm into the sleeve. Then she eased Hayden into his arms, patting him on the back when he whimpered.

"It's okay," she whispered. "Sleep well, buddy." She stepped back, clasping her hands behind her. "Good night, Nate."

At least <u>she</u> was being smart.

That made one of them. He took a small step toward her and bent to kiss her, lightly. "Thanks, Lucie." He straightened and made for the back door. Silence. Maybe he'd surprised her as much as he'd surprised himself, he mused as he exited the house.

She tasted sweet, warm. And he really needed to get a grip on his self-control.

Chapter Five

E asier said than done.

He steeled himself when Hayden shrieked her name as he raced into the mudroom the next morning. He heard her low murmur when his son opened the door, then a quiet laugh. He'd spent half the night wondering what it would be like to really kiss her. It had been a long time since he'd kissed a woman. Not since Greta left.

Maybe kissing Lucie wasn't such a terrible idea. She wasn't staying. He could give in to the urge, and then forget about it after she was gone.

And dammit, he wanted to kiss her. Blowing out a hard breath, he rinsed Hayden's juice glass and shut off the faucet as their footsteps neared. He glanced over and watched her cheeks turn pink. "Hi."

"Daddy, can we play outside later?"

He blinked and turned his attention to his son. "I'll try, buddy, but–"

"I meant Lucie an' me." Hayden gave him a quick frown. "It's sunny out."

"And I bet the grass is crunchy, too." He met Lucie's

gaze, restraining a smile at her nod and his son's subsequent down-turned mouth. "Maybe we can talk about it at lunchtime after I get some things done."

His son pursed his lips, blue eyes narrowed as he studied his father for a few seconds. "Okay."

"It's actually pretty chilly out this morning," Lucie said. "I had to get my really heavy sweater out. I'll have to get my coat out soon."

Hayden looked up at her. "Really?"

She tugged at the collar of the thick green sweater she wore.

The little boy heaved a giant sigh. "Okay." He released her hand. "I gotta get my bear." He ran out of the kitchen.

"Slow on the stairs, buddy!" Nate called.

"'Kay!"

Lucie winced while she listened to his footsteps rushing up the steps.

Nate set the juice glass down and crossed the floor to where she stood. "I need to know," he said, bending to catch her soft mouth with his.

She made a startled sound, then set both of her hands flat on his chest, her lips parting.

He'd been right. She tasted sweet. He slid one hand into her loose hair, ignoring the slight dampness to tip her head so he could delve deeper.

She let him. God, she let him.

He pulled back, his heart knocking hard against his ribs. Lucie's eyes opened slowly, and he noted the way they had darkened. "Tell me I'm being stupid."

"Maybe we both are," she said huskily, a faint smile curving her puffy lips. "I haven't been stupid in a long time, and right now, I have no idea why."

"Shit." He dragged in a rough breath. "One of us should be smart, right?"

She shook her head. "I'm tired of being the smart one." Her fingers slid up to his shoulders, cautiously, warm through his cotton shirt. "Being the smart one got me dumped with no warning, being smart left me jobless." Her smile widened. "Though that got me here, so that's something."

Nate's fingers tightened on her hip. When had he grabbed her hip? He loosened his grasp. "You're not staying, so it wouldn't be smart for us to do this. I'm not looking for a relationship. I have all I can handle with Hayden and my business."

"Then this might be just exactly what we both need. Something temporary." Her eyes rounded, and her smile faded. "I've never tried temporary until I came here."

He'd *never* tried it. Not knowingly, anyway. "Maybe..." He broke off at the sound of running footsteps upstairs. "Slow down, buddy."

Lucie startled, then stepped away, blushing.

Hayden jumped down from the next to last step, his bear in a death grip in his arms. "I'm ready."

"Almost," Lucie said. "You need your jacket."

His son heaved another dramatic sigh, but didn't argue.

Nate's eyebrows went up. If he'd said that, his son would probably have made some protest, or at least a small attempt to wheedle. Hayden liked Lucie. While his son collected his jacket from the mud room, Nate met Lucie's gaze. "You'd let me know if he was misbehaving, right?"

She smiled again. "Of course. But he's been good, even at naptime."

Hayden held out his bear. "Daddy, hold 'im so I can get my coat on."

Lucie helped with the jacket, zipping it up to his son's

chin, then tweaking his nose so he giggled. "Are you sure you only need Mr. Cuddles?"

"Yep." He took the bear back, and Nate crouched to give him a quick hug. "I know, Daddy, I'll be a good boy."

Nate smiled. "Glad to hear it. I'll see you around lunchtime." He nodded at Lucie. "Thank you."

She flushed pink. "We'll see you later, Nate."

He followed them into the mud room and grabbed a flannel shirt that would serve as a jacket for his short walk to the workshop. "If you need anything, I'll be in the shop."

Not thinking about how she'd kissed him back. No, he'd be busy finishing the Wells' new kitchen cabinets. Way too busy to think about how soft and warm her lips were under his, how she'd felt against him.

The door closed behind them, and he squeezed his eyes shut. *Shit.*

———

EVERY TIME HE FOUND HIMSELF THINKING ABOUT THE KISS, Nate redirected his thoughts to his to-do list for the day. Finish these cabinets. Build the ramp at his parents' house. Figure out a vehicle to bring Dad home from the hospital tomorrow. That got him through most of the morning. When he stopped over to check on Lucie and Hayden, they were coloring. Instead of lingering, he grabbed some lumber and plywood from the shop and loaded it into the back of the truck with his saw and tape measure. Time to build a ramp.

By the time he'd constructed a sturdy ramp to the front porch, it was well after lunchtime. He stood inside his parents' kitchen, looking out at his dad's shop. He could run back to the house and check on Hayden before heading to the hospital.

Or he could avoid temptation and just get on the ferry now.

He took his cell phone out and pulled up Lucie's number. "Hi."

"Hi. I wanted to check in and make sure you're okay before I go to the hospital."

"Fine. Hayden is sleeping. He played hard this morning, so it only took a couple minutes before he was out." He heard the smile in her voice. "He kept waving to the lighthouse, waving so hard I thought his arm would fall off."

"Waving to Micah."

"That's what he said."

Nate hesitated. "Micah is a ghost."

For a moment, there was silence. "What?"

He grinned. "Micah is the ghost of a lightkeeper who lived there about a hundred years ago."

Lucie remained silent again, longer this time. "But I saw him," she said finally. "When I was walking last week. I thought it was you up there, and I waved. You...he...waved back..." Her voice trailed off.

"You've seen him more than once." He knew she'd seen him one day when he'd been taking Hayden to his parents'.

"I thought..."

When she didn't continue, he cleared his throat. Maybe this wasn't really a phone conversation. "I'm sorry, I should have waited to tell you."

"It's fine," she said faintly.

"I'll tell you the story later. I just wanted to check in before I get on the ferry, not to freak you out." He glanced at the clock over the sink. He needed to move if he wanted to catch the next ferry. "I'll be back earlier today, I promise. Call if you need anything."

"Okay, thanks, Nate." The call disconnected.

He was an idiot. He stuffed his phone in his pocket and headed for the truck.

———

Lucie stood at the kitchen sink, staring up at the lighthouse where the man stood. No, not a man, a ghost. She swallowed. She wasn't sure she believed in ghosts. She'd never had any brushes with them before, anyway. She squeezed her eyes shut and shook her head. He must be kidding. She opened her eyes and looked up again. No one there.

She turned away from the window. She needed to figure out dinner. And finish the lunch clean-up. She didn't want to wonder about ghosts. So she didn't. She washed up the few dishes from their lunch, mentally inventorying the contents of the fridge and freezer.

But her gaze strayed back to the lighthouse as she dried her hands. No one visible in the windows at the top of the tower. Uneasy, she turned away. Dinner. That's what she wanted to think about.

After a quick rummage through the fridge, she started cleaning and chopping vegetables. A nice hearty soup for supper. While the veggies simmered, she mixed up a quick loaf of bread and set it aside to rise.

"Hey, Lucie."

She smiled as she turned around to find Hayden emerging from the hallway to the bedrooms, rubbing one little fist against his eye and dragging his bear in his other hand. "Did you have a good rest?"

He nodded. "Mr. Cuddles heard a noise and woke me up. Whatcha doin'?"

"Working on supper. I have soup started and some bread.

What do you think we should do for dessert?"

He shrugged, yawning.

She poured a small cup of juice and put it on the table. "I was thinking about an apple crisp. Do you like those?"

"Prob'ly. I don' know what that is." He climbed up onto a chair at the table and leaned his head on his hand. "You make good food, Lucie."

"Well, thank you." She sat, too. "We have some time before I need to put the meat into the soup. What do you want to do?" She watched his sleepy blue eyes as he tried to focus.

"Nothin' yet." He reached for the cup, and took a sip of the juice. "Mr. Cuddles shoulda let me sleep a few more minutes."

She hid a grin and ruffled his messy hair. "Maybe he should have. You take your time, buddy."

While she chopped apples and mixed up the other ingredients, he stayed at the table, drinking his juice and talking quietly to his bear. "Lucie?"

She poured the mixture into her baking pan. "Yes?"

"Mr. Micah looked sad today."

She blinked. "How could you tell from so far away?" she asked after a moment.

"His shoulders were down. Like this." He demonstrated, slumping his little shoulders forward.

"Hm." She slid the crisp into the oven and set the timer. "Have you seen him closer?"

Hayden frowned. "Lotsa times."

"Does he talk to you?"

"I dunno. I can't hear him up there."

"I thought you saw him closer?"

"He comes in Daddy's shop sometimes, but he doesn't talk there." His shoulders lifted in a shrug.

Lucie wasn't sure how to ask anything further. At least

not with a three year-old. "Are you awake yet?"

He grinned. "Yes. Can we read the big book in the bedroom?"

She nodded. "Why don't you get it while I give the soup a stir." No more ghost talk for now.

Nate arrived just after she'd dished up soup and bread, so instead of sitting down, she grabbed another bowl and spoon. "Sit down. I'll be right back," she said, turning to the stove.

He bent to kiss his son's head and shed his heavy jacket. "Thank you, Lucie."

She brought his soup as he dropped onto the chair on the other side of his son from where she'd put her own dinner. Without thinking, she smoothed his rumpled hair down, as she'd done earlier for Hayden.

His dark eyes locked on her face, and she snatched her hand away, flushing. "Sorry," she muttered, going to her chair. Luckily, Hayden was already slurping soup and didn't notice.

Between bites of warm bread and spoonfuls of the thick stew, the little boy chattered to his father, allowing Lucie to pull herself together while pretending to eat her own meal. Finally, when Hayden took a break to stuff the last of his bread into his mouth, she cleared her throat.

"Is your dad ready to come home?"

Nate nodded. "I just have to figure out how we're going to transport him."

She frowned, then realized Nate only had the pick-up truck. That wouldn't work. "You know," she said slowly, "Harry and Mindi left their SUV for a 'just in case'. I bet you could put him in there and bring him home comfortably."

He frowned.

"The backseat's on rails, and it slides back, so he'll have room for his leg." She smiled.

"That might work." He studied his bowl, thinking.

She didn't press, instead putting another spoonful of soup into her mouth.

"I'm ready for dessert, Lucie," Hayden said as his spoon clinked against his empty bowl.

"How about if we wait until Lucie is ready, too, buddy?" Nate winked at his son, who smiled.

She blushed. "I'm almost done." She finished her last bite of stew and pushed away from the table.

Nate rose, too, gathering his son's dishes. "Let me get these."

She didn't protest, but went to the oven and pulled out the warm pan.

"It smells good, Lucie!" Hayden shouted.

"It does, but how about your inside voice, buddy?" Nate rinsed out the bowls while she dished out apple crisp, then put whipped cream on top of each plate. "That looks as good as it smells," he murmured, stepping closer. "I can help."

"Better get the first one to Hayden." She saw the little boy's grin widen.

"I suppose I should." He took a plate and fork with him, and she followed with the other two.

Dessert was punctuated with more chatter and giggles from Hayden's side of the table. "I wanna Lucie restaurant," he announced while he scraped the last of the whipped cream from his empty plate.

She blinked. "I think you're in one right now," she teased.

His mouth twisted. "No, a *real* restaurant. You should do it, Lucie."

"I don't know how to run a restaurant, Hayden."

"You just cook, an' people come eat."

"I bet you could find someone who does know, for advice." Nate tapped his own fork against his empty plate.

"You should at least go look at the restaurant while you're looking at job listings. Unless you found something already."

She shook her head slowly. A restaurant of her own. Her pulse skipped a beat. She couldn't possibly do that. She didn't know the first thing about running a restaurant.

"We can get Stu to let you take a look at the old Jenny's Restaurant. He's off-island to see his son in Augusta, but he'll be back soon. It can't hurt just to go look."

Her eyes widened. "Um..." She bit her lower lip for a second. "I don't know if I could pull that off."

"What was your job? Before the company was bought and moved?"

She slid a sidelong glance at him. "I developed sales training programs for an electronics company."

His eyebrows lifted. "Wow, you gave up being a cook in your own restaurant for that, huh?" he teased.

She smiled reluctantly. "I know. But getting a business degree made my parents happy."

"Did your job make you happy?"

She shrugged. "It let me pay the bills and put money away. I worked with some good people."

"What will make *you* happy?"

She blinked. "I don't know."

He touched her wrist. "Maybe you should think about it."

She glanced down at his long fingers. "I guess."

He laughed. "That wasn't very enthusiastic. I'll call Stu and set up a time. No strings. You don't have to do it, it's just an option."

"Why?"

"Why not?"

She frowned at Nate. "I..." It seemed silly to argue. She could look at it and keep up her real job search. "I'll think about it."

He smiled a little, as if he knew what she was thinking.

She dragged her gaze back to her dessert plate. He didn't know what she was thinking, she was being silly.

"Daddy, you gotta look at my pictures."

"After we clear the table, Hayden."

She scooped up the last bite of her dessert. "I'm all done. Let me get–"

"I can do the dishes." Nate pushed his chair back and stood, collecting his son's plate and fork, stacking it with his own, and then hers.

"You don't have to do that. There aren't that many, it'll only take me a few minutes."

He leveled a stern look at her. "I will do them. You made dinner."

She sighed. "Thank you."

His mouth softened. "No, thank you, Lucie. I really appreciate you keeping Hayden the last few days."

"It's been fun." She looked over at Hayden, who watched them. "Get your pictures to show your Daddy." She helped him out of the booster seat, and he ran into the next room.

While Nate washed the dishes, she put away the leftovers, packing the stew away into the freezer, and the apple crisp into a small container she could send home with Nate and Hayden. Nate turned to her, drying his hands, after he'd finished his self-appointed chore.

"I told you earlier we'd talk about Micah."

She looked up from the pages Hayden had spread across the table. She'd forgotten.

"Maybe we could talk over at our place. Let Hayden start to wind down before bedtime."

Lucie nodded. "Sure." She wanted to hear this ghost story.

Nate got Hayden into his pajamas, and then his son settled on the floor in his room with several trucks spread around him. Lucie waited downstairs, and he wondered what her reaction would be now that she'd had some time to think about the lighthouse ghost. He descended the steps and found her perched on the sofa. "I think there might be wine in the fridge if you'd like some. Mom brings a bottle occasionally, just so the house is supplied for company."

She shook her head. "I'm good, thanks."

He crossed the room and sat down across from her in his comfortable armchair. "So, Micah..."

Her eyes narrowed.

He cleared his throat. "In the eighteen-eighties, Micah MacDonald moved here to become the light-keeper, after his brother died in a boating accident. He'd met the very beautiful Lucinda Webster on the mainland shortly before and fallen in love. She thought living in a lighthouse would be romantic, so she chose Micah from an apparently crowded field of suitors." He leaned forward, resting his elbows on his knees. "Not exactly the best reason, but Micah was in love so he probably believed she was, too."

"She was young, I suppose." A faint line appeared between Lucie's eyebrows.

"Probably. Anyway, they married and moved into the lighthouse. For a few years, things were fine by all accounts. Eventually, Lucinda decided she was bored and lonely in the lighthouse. Micah loved her still, so when she wanted to travel to visit her parents on the mainland, he made the arrangements. She was only gone a couple of weeks, but when she came back, she was even more unhappy."

"She saw all the things she was missing," Lucie guessed.

He shrugged. "Maybe. Soon after she returned, a man arrived on the island. Micah didn't know him, but evidently Lucinda did, from before their marriage. The story goes that she reconnected with him while visiting her parents, and decided that she loved him instead of her husband. So he came to the island to collect Lucinda. She packed a small bag and went up to the top of the lighthouse, where Micah was working at the time. She told him she was leaving the island, leaving him." He stopped, noting the sadness in Lucie's eyes. "Micah loved his wife, so he tried to stop her, to persuade her to stay, but she wouldn't listen. She rushed down the steps and outside, where her new love waited. Micah hurried after her, but he tripped and tumbled down the stairs. The fall killed him. Lucinda and her new love fled without telling anyone what had happened."

Two big, fat tears slid down Lucie's face, and she swiped them away. "That's awful."

He agreed. "Micah stayed, though. Shortly after his body was found by his brother-in-law, he started appearing in the lighthouse and his house, which is now the back room of my wood-shop. The new light-keeper saw him first, just a few weeks after he arrived. As more people came to live on the island, more sightings happened. Even after the lighthouse was automated and no light-keeper lived there, he remained."

"Waiting for her to come home?" There was a hitch in the question as she wiped away more tears.

Nate shrugged again. "I didn't mean to upset you."

She shook her head. "I'm fine."

That was a lie. Several more tears slid down her face.

"Really." She smiled as she brushed her fingers across her wet cheeks. "It's just a sad story. I hope Lucinda and her new love at least had a happy ending."

He hesitated.

"Oh no. What?"

He tried to think of a way to avoid telling her the rest. He'd already made her cry.

"You have to finish the story, Nate." She frowned at him.

He blew out a hard breath. "Her new love turned out to not be such a nice guy. He and some family valuables went missing at the same time, then he came back to her parents' a few days later. They had an argument, and it got physical according to her mother. Lucinda slapped him more than once, and he hit her back, harder. She took a tumble down the stairs and broke her neck. He ended up hanging for it."

Lucie sat back on the sofa, eyes wide. "That's horrible."

He nodded.

She bit her lip for a second. "On the other hand, if Micah didn't get his happy ending, I suppose it's only fair Lucinda didn't either. Poor Micah." She sniffed and rubbed one cheek dry. "I'm sorry."

"Why?"

"For crying and making you uncomfortable."

"I'm not." He wasn't, he realized. He should be.

She smiled. "Well, that's a relief." She pushed to her feet. "I'm going to go so you can get Hayden settled. I'll see you guys in the morning again?"

He rose and caught her hand.

She went still, her pretty eyes widening as she looked up.

"I want you to know I really do appreciate your help, Lucie. I don't know what I would have done the last few days without it." Her warm fingers relaxed in his. "Can I kiss you good-night?"

She tilted her head. "Are you sure?"

He tugged on her hand as he stepped closer. "Positive."

She tipped her chin higher, smiling as her cheeks

pinkened. "Then my answer is yes." She set her free hand on his jaw and rose on tiptoe.

Nate brushed her lips with his, lightly. When hers parted, he dipped in for a better taste. Her tongue met his, tentatively, and he groaned before he could stop himself, using his free hand to catch her nape and pull her closer.

Lucie pressed nearer still, her fingers warm on his cheek.

He took full advantage, kissing her until he had to release her mouth to drag in a quick lungful of air. When he opened his eyes, he noted her flushed cheeks, her puffy wet mouth, her long lashes fluttering up to reveal dark green eyes filled with need.

He wanted more.

She slid her hand to his nape, and he shivered, aware of his erection pressing into her belly, of her tight nipples against his chest. The way her ragged breathing matched his own. She wanted more, too. He stroked his thumb along her lower lip, and her eyes closed for a second.

Then she swallowed and touched her tongue to the tip of his thumb, holding his gaze.

He released her other hand and grabbed her hip to pull her nearer.

She obliged, lifting higher on her toes.

"Lucie."

She bit her lip. "I know. Not a good time." Her eyes squeezed shut.

"I was thinking maybe we could both get Hayden to bed." It was a terrible idea, asking her to stay.

But the way her eyes lit up made him ignore that. "And then?"

"And then..." He didn't go further. He didn't want to pressure her. Or himself.

But he sure as hell didn't want her to leave now.

Chapter Six

Lucie walked upstairs ahead of Nate, aware of his gaze on her back. Too aware, of that and of what might be coming soon. Heat washed through her. *Stop it.* She needed to think about story time first. She smiled. Story time would be fun.

Hayden looked up from his trucks when she stepped into the room. "Hi, Lucie. My trucks are driving home."

She knelt nearby. "Good timing, since it's story time."

He frowned for a second, then looked up at his dad. "Can you both read a story?"

She bit her lip and glanced over her shoulder at Nate, whose eyes crinkled at the corners, as if he was also suppressing a smile.

"That depends on how long the stories are, buddy," he said.

The little boy sighed. "All right." He picked up his trucks and carried them to the toy box on the other side of the room. "I'll pick 'em."

Lucie sat cross-legged on the floor while he perused the small shelf near his bed. After a few moments, he chose two books, the big story collection she'd read from the first night, and a single story. He gave her the big book and carried the other to his father, who sat on the rocking chair.

"Daddy, you read this one. Lucie, you can read my favorite one after."

She swallowed. "Sure."

Nate settled his son on his lap and opened his book, clearing his throat. Hayden giggled through the story about the trio cats trying to find their way home, making his father stop several times so he could look closer at the pictures.

Lucie relaxed, watching them. Nate was a great dad.

By the time the story was over, Hayden's eyes drooped. "Now you, Lucie," he said as his father closed his book.

"Okay." She paged through the bigger book to his story and began reading. About halfway through, he struggled to keep his eyes open. His lashes fluttered shut for several seconds, then lifted again, before repeating. By the time she finished, he was sound asleep. She smiled and shut her book, pushing to her feet and holding out her hand for the one Nate still held.

He gave it to her and rose, crossing to the bed to tuck his son in. She put the books back on the shelf and headed for the door, glancing back to see Nate brushing a kiss on Hayden's cheek.

Her pulse kicked up a gear as he turned around. His expression shifted when his gaze landed on her. His eyes darkened, and she flushed in response. She took a quick breath and moved into the hallway, toward the stairs.

His slow, quiet footfalls on the carpet runner behind her made her heart pound faster with each step down. By the time she reached the living room, her pulse drowned out anything else in her head.

Nate's fingers settled on her shoulder when she stopped

walking in the middle of the living room. She sucked in a quick breath, then turned to face him.

He studied her expression so long she wondered what he was looking for, what he saw. She stepped closer, and his eyes darkened a little more.

"Just for now," she whispered, stretching up on tiptoe, sliding her hands up his wide chest to his shoulders.

His jaw tightened, but he bent to her.

The man could kiss. Deep and slow, warm and soft. Harder, so she pressed nearer. His hands held her tight, one at her hip, the other in the middle of her back. Even when they had to part for air, it was only briefly, just a heartbeat, until he caught her mouth again.

She had no idea how long they stood there. It didn't matter. She didn't want it to end. It felt good to be wanted. Eventually, she realized how much more she wanted. His erection was a new temptation against her belly. His fingers cupping her ass, squeezing, sent molten heat to her core, and she rocked against him.

He groaned, so she did it again, feeling a rush of pleasure at being the cause.

He hauled her up, and she wrapped one leg around his waist. God, that felt good, *so good*, when he pressed his hips tighter against her.

She gasped into his kiss when she suddenly tilted, then realized he'd turned and carried her down onto the sofa beneath him.

Better.

He slipped one hand under the hem of her sweater, rough, warm fingers brushing her belly before they lifted to stroke the underside of her breast.

"Oh!"

His head lifted just a little. "Yes?"

"God, yes." She made her fingers release the death grip she had on his shoulders, smiling. "Please."

Nate smiled, too, a wicked, slow curve of his mouth as he rubbed one finger over her nipple.

The rush of heat inside her started there and ended at the point where his cock pressed between her thighs.

His smile faded. "I want to put my mouth on you, Lucie." He punctuated the gruff statement with another stroke.

Her limbs went heavy at the desire in his dark eyes and the corresponding rush of need that bloomed inside her.

"I want to see you. I want to touch you." He leaned down and planted a hard kiss on her mouth.

She slid one hand to his nape, threading her fingers through his hair to hold him when he would have lifted his head. "I want that, too," she whispered against his mouth, watching heat flare in his eyes.

His kiss this time was rough, hungry, demanding, and she let him take what he wanted, because she wanted it, too.

———

NATE TRIED TO REMIND HIMSELF TO BE PATIENT, TO TAKE HIS time. It had been a long time, for both of them. But Lucie's responses were so open, so unguarded and natural, he couldn't help himself.

He eased her sweater up, up, until her cotton and lace bra came into view, her nipple dark against the thin white fabric. His mouth watered, and he bent to touch his tongue to her, through the lingerie.

She made a strangled sound, her fingers tightening in his hair for a second, before she released him and yanked her sweater off over her head.

He groaned. "So pretty, Lucie," he rasped, his gaze sliding up to meet hers. "You're so pretty."

The pink in her cheeks deepened, and a shy smile touched her mouth. "Thank you."

He swallowed and let his gaze drift back down to her breasts. The bra hooked in the front, conveniently. He flipped it open and peeled it away from her pale flesh, noting the way her breathing hitched. Pretty pink nipples puckered tight, and he bent to brush his lips over one.

Her gasp warmed the top of his head.

He parted his lips to catch the sweet bit of flesh, laving the tip with his tongue so her hips jerked up. *Fuck.* His imagination went into overdrive, and his dick throbbed harder. If he wasn't careful, he'd lose control. He was out of practice.

Lucie arched up to meet him when he bent to her other nipple, and he couldn't stop the way his hips ground into hers. Her soft moan encouraged him to do it again, and she rubbed along the length of his cock.

Shit.

Nate slid one hand under her to hold her there, and she whimpered. "It's okay, Lucie," he breathed against her skin, pressing kisses around her nipple, teasing them both.

"Please, Nate." Her leg tightened around his waist, and his brain brought up an image of being buried deep inside her, of heat and wetness wrapped around him.

He licked the bit of dark rose flesh, watching it pucker tighter, and then sucked it into his mouth. Perfect. Her nails dragged along his scalp, and she lifted into him. He took more of her breast in, sucking lightly, then harder, scraping with the edge of his teeth so she shuddered under him.

Her hips rocked into his, harder, faster.

He didn't want to rush. He didn't. But he needed to know...

He slipped his hand from her ass to the button and zipper at the front of her jeans, easing his fingers inside. They brushed lace, then cotton. He retraced, and found his way into her panties. Down, down through crisp hair, lower to her slick sex.

Lucie moaned, and her legs loosened around his waist, falling open wider.

Perfect. Better access. He brushed one finger into her wet flesh.

Jesus. So wet.

He pressed deeper, and her inner muscles clenched on his finger. So tight.

"Oh, Nate, please."

He stretched to kiss her, and he stroked up to find her clit instead of pressing inside her again. She jolted at the first stroke, then met the next. He rubbed slowly, testing different strokes, pressures to find what she liked best. Slow and hard, light and quick, a gentle pinch, a harder twist, and, unexpectedly, she came apart beneath him, stifling a cry in his shoulder. She trembled, her breath ragged.

Nate slid his fingers lower and discovered she was far wetter now. He pressed two fingers inside her to feel her orgasm. Her pussy clenched tight around him. So good.

"Please, Nate, please, Nate," she whispered.

He kissed her again. Dimly, he realized she was fumbling with his shirt buttons, his jeans. He should help her, but when her warm fingers grazed his skin, his chest, his belly, all he could think about was getting inside her. She brushed her fingertips over the head of his erection, and his mind blanked on everything but *more*. And *now*.

It took him several long moments to realize he needed air. Needed to breathe. When he managed it, Lucie had shoved his jeans and underwear down and wrapped her hand around him. "Shit," he growled.

She kissed his chin, then his jaw. "Please, Nate."

He dragged in a longer breath and held it for a second, then released it, slowly. "I have a condom in my wallet," he managed.

Her other hand slid around to his ass, stroking, then down to his jeans. She fumbled for his pocket until she snagged his wallet and presented it to him.

He nipped at her lower lip, then took the wallet, flipping it open. He found the condom and tossed the wallet aside. "You need to be naked, sweetheart. I haven't seen all of you yet, and I want to feel you under me."

She blushed. "You aren't naked either."

"You have a point." Reluctantly, he eased his fingers out of her, then shoved up onto his knees. He shrugged off his open shirt, then got to his feet so he could strip off his jeans and underwear. When he bent to pull off her sneakers, he realized her gaze had latched onto his cock. He discarded her shoes, trying to ignore the heat of her gaze, then tugged her jeans and panties off. "Oh, look at you," he murmured, sliding one hand up the inside of her leg. "So pretty." Her muscles tightened a tiny bit, and he met her gaze. "Easy, Lucie."

She shivered, but her thighs relaxed.

He knelt beside the sofa, bending to kiss her. The taste of her was addicting. Sweet and warm, with a darker flavor beneath. Tempting. He let his fingers continue to slip up her leg, finding her wet folds, the sensitive bit of flesh within.

Her hands skated across his chest, down his ribs to his belly. He tensed in anticipation and wasn't disappointed when she stroked one finger along his erection. When she squeezed, he grunted, rocking toward her.

"Please, Nate," she repeated against his mouth. "Come inside me. I'm dying here."

He smiled. "Well, I'd hate for that to happen." He flicked his thumb over her clit just to see her eyes darken. To feel the fresh rush of wetness on his fingers.

She dragged her fingers up the length of his cock, then down.

Yes.

He tore open the packet and gently nudged her fingers off of him before he rolled the condom onto himself, then scooped her up. He sat and eased her down over him, holding her poised just above his erection.

Her nails dug into his shoulders.

Her pretty eyes were dark with need, and he held her gaze while he pressed inside her. Her lips parted on a silent gasp, and he pulled her closer, so her hard little nipples pressed into his chest, rubbing down as he settled her lower, lower, until he was fully inside her. *God.*

She shuddered, but her gaze stayed locked on his face. "Nate."

He nudged her nose with his. "You feel so good, Lucie." She did, tight and wet and hot all around him, her warm skin pressed along his, smooth where his was roughened with hair. He leaned in to kiss her lightly.

But she was done with easy, evidently. She slid both hands into his hair to pull him back when he started to ease away, her wet, swollen lips brushing his, pressing his open so she could taste. And her inner muscles clenched around him. *Fuck.*

He caught one of her breasts in his hand, giving a gentle squeeze before he pinched the tip. She arched toward him, her hips shifting. Reminding him he had two hands. He wedged his free hand between them so he could stroke her clit.

Lucie began to move, rocking up and back down the length of him. He wasn't ready. God, that felt good. So damn good. He let her continue, concentrating on her reactions to his touch.

She rocked faster, and his need grew more desperate. His hips lifted to meet hers, without his consent. Again.

He loved the soft, needy sounds she made, whimpers and moans. They tasted good. So did her breast, which he bent to when she arched in response to the harder stroke he gave her clit.

"I need...oh, God," she whispered. Her pussy tightened on him, hard.

"I know." He nibbled his way to her other breast, using his teeth and tongue to make her moan, his fingers on her clit to jolt her into a faster rhythm. "It's okay, sweetheart. Let go again."

She shook her head, but more wetness met his fingers. Fuck, he wanted to feel that on his bare cock. He flipped her under him on the sofa, startling her so she muffled a cry in his chest. And he stroked into her faster now. Harder. He needed to know how she felt around him when she came.

Her breaths came quick and shallow, hot against his cheek, his throat, and her thighs tightened at his hips. "Oh, God. Nate, I...oh!" She bit her lower lip, and he groaned at the rush of pleasure when her orgasm burst, tight and wet, fuck, so wet around him. Her body bowed toward him, every muscle tensed.

He nipped at her collarbone, trying to slow his breathing. But his body was there, too. Past the point of no return. His own release exploded free, his balls tightening so pleasure rocketed through him.

Better than he'd imagined. Better than anything he'd ever imagined.

He braced himself on his elbows beside her shoulders and caught her mouth roughly.

It was a long time before his brain was functional, and it came back slowly. He realized they were both slick with sweat, that he was probably crushing her into the sofa, his forehead resting on the cushion beside her. That her breathing was still accelerated, but not as fast as a few minutes ago.

Her warm fingers skated up and down his spine, prolonging the pleasure, sending fresh bursts of heat along his skin.

He turned his head to look at her in the dim light. Her eyes were closed now, dark hair damp around her face, lips puffy, and her skin still flushed. After a moment, her lashes fluttered up, and she turned to meet his gaze.

"Wow." A faint smile touched her mouth.

"I'll second that." He grinned.

She inhaled slowly, then released the air, stroking one hand from his cheek to his hair.

He shut his eyes for a second. "That feels good." It did. It had been a long time since anyone besides family touched him.

She continued, and he relaxed. Not entirely. He needed to get up soon to get rid of the condom. But he enjoyed her touch for several more minutes. Eventually, though, he pressed a kiss on her jaw. "I have to get up," he murmured.

She didn't protest, but he saw her tiny wince when he withdrew from her. He felt the same way, but this was necessary. He picked up his underwear and padded into the downstairs bathroom.

His reflection in the mirror over the sink reflected a man

he hadn't seen in a long time–rumpled and satisfied. He looked away and cleaned up quickly.

By the time he returned to the living room, Lucie was half-dressed. He frowned.

She blushed. "I thought..." She bit her lip. "I figured you have to get up early, and I can't be here when Hayden gets up."

She had a point. But if he was honest, somewhere in his mind, he'd imagined more. Like the rest of the night. Waking early to kiss her awake. "I suppose." He tried to erase his scowl, but wasn't sure he succeeded. He sat on the coffee table in front of her, noting the way her flush deepened when his gaze flicked down to her bare legs. He stroked her knee. "I know." He sighed. It was just sex. That was all it could be. He lived here. She didn't. Period. "But I would like to kiss you again."

She smiled. "If you do that, I might not think leaving is such a good idea."

"There are more condoms in my bathroom cupboard," he said, letting his fingers slide up her thigh a few inches.

Her eyes darkened. "Maybe we can use another one tomorrow."

Her husky whisper went right to his dick. "That far away?" he teased.

She inhaled shakily. "Yes, I think so." She picked up her jeans and got to her feet.

Her legs seemed a mile long, then disappeared into the faded blue denim she tugged up, leaving him staring.

Lucie laughed, touching his jaw. "You're going to make me forget my good intentions."

He shoved to his feet and bent to kiss her, hard and quick. His own good intentions were fading fast.

She licked her lips, eyes dazed. "I need to go."

He knew she was right, so he turned and found her sneakers, handing them over.

In under a minute, she stood in front of him, cheeks pink, looking as if she might run.

Nate took a slow breath. "I'll find out in the morning when they're discharging Dad."

She nodded. "I can keep Hayden while you work, if there's time to work before you have to leave."

He brushed her hair away from her cheek. "Sleep well, Lucie."

She smiled again. "You, too." She turned and headed for the mud room, and he followed, not bothering to stop looking at her ass this time. She paused at the back door, then glanced over her shoulder.

Nate leaned in and kissed her, softly. "Good night."

She reached up to touch his cheek, smiling, then stepped outside.

He waited until the back light next door went off before he shut off his own and locked the door. He stood there in the dark for a moment. Maybe sex with Lucie wasn't a good idea, but it had felt damn good.

And he wanted to do it again.

Chapter Seven

L ucie shivered when she opened the back door in the morning. "Whoa!"

Nate laughed. "It got a little chilly last night."

"I got my heavy coat on!" Hayden shouted.

She looked down. "Nice. I like the dogs."

He rushed inside. "Daddy said I had to."

His father came inside, too, and closed the door. "That's what happens when fall comes, buddy. Warm coats for cold days." He met her gaze, and she felt heat in her cheeks. "Hi."

"Hi." She swallowed.

"I talked to Mom. She hasn't got a straight answer from anyone, so it seems like they're not in a hurry to discharge Dad."

"Then you work this morning." Her fingers itched to touch his clean-shaven jaw, but she didn't.

"I got the zipper down, Daddy!"

She looked away from Nate. That was why. She shouldn't touch Nate in front of Hayden. She didn't want to confuse him. "That's great."

"It's gettin' easy now I'm a big boy." He flung his coat at

one of the kitchen chairs. "I got up real early this mornin', Lucie. It was dark."

And *that* was why she couldn't spend the night. "Well, you know day-time is getting shorter now, too, buddy. Winter is coming." She took a quick breath. "I have plans for you this morning."

"Yay!" He jumped up and down a couple of times, then ran into the living room.

She blushed as she turned to Nate. "You have work, right?"

"You kicking me out again?" A slow grin tugged at one corner of his mouth.

Her face flamed hotter. "No, of course not."

He touched her cheek with his forefinger. "I do have work to do. I'll let you know as soon as I hear from Mom." His gaze slid past her for a second. "Have a good time, buddy."

"I will, Daddy!"

Lucie inhaled slowly as he exited, then turned to face Hayden. "I was thinking about making brownies this morning. Maybe your Grandpa would like something to cheer him up when he gets home."

"I bet he would." The little boy frowned. "Are you givin' 'em all to Grampa?"

She laughed. "I could save one or two for you."

He cheered. "I like brownies."

"I thought you might feel that way. Come on, let's get started. I thought we could make dinner for your Grandpa and Grandma, too."

"I'll help."

She didn't tell him she'd already chopped vegetables and the chicken she'd cooked when she got up early, too wired to sleep. "Okay, sounds good."

By the time they finished mixing up the batter for the brownies, the casserole was done, so she swapped baking pans, covering the casserole on top of the stove. "How about we read while the brownies bake, and then we'll go outside to play?"

"Okay! I'll get the books." Hayden hurried into the living room.

Lucie put the bowl and spoons into the dishwasher, and turned that on, then headed for the next room, where he waited with a small stack of books on the sofa. She smiled and dropped down beside him. He snuggled closer and handed over the books. She hugged him. "Which one is first?"

He pointed to the top book, and she flipped it open.

They'd read all four books by the time the brownies were ready to come out of the oven. "Can you get your coat on, or do you need help with the zipper, buddy?"

"I got it."

"Okay." She plucked her own coat from the rack inside the door and buttoned it up. When he struggled for a few seconds with the zipper, then shot her a doleful look, she knelt to help.

The brisk wind stole her breath when they moved away from the protection of the house. "Wow!" She turned her collar up around her neck and reached for his hood. "I think your ears might freeze and fall off unless we cover them up, Hayden."

Just as she'd hoped, he laughed but didn't protest.

They played for almost an hour, until Hayden's teeth started chattering. "I'm not c-cold," he insisted.

"Maybe you're not, but I'm frozen. And I'm thinking about some hot chocolate to go with a couple of those brownies. Do you like hot chocolate?"

"Yes!" He ran toward the house, protest forgotten in the eye of a double-helping of chocolate.

Smiling, she followed him inside, shedding her coat and pouring some milk into a small pot before he'd gotten his coat off. By the time he'd hung it up and washed his hands, she had cocoa powder and some baking chocolate out, two mugs waiting on the counter, and two brownies on napkins on the table.

Lucie rubbed her cold hands together, watching Hayden climb onto the chair closest to her. "We'll have hot chocolate in a few minutes." She glanced at the pot. The milk was just getting to the tiny bubble stage. "I might even have whipped cream left to put on top."

He cheered.

Smiling, she turned off the burner, then grated some of the chocolate in, whisking until it had melted into the hot milk. Next up was the cocoa powder, and she stirred until the contents of the pot were dark and thicker. She poured some into the small, sturdy mug and dug into the fridge for the whipped cream before presenting the mug to Hayden.

"Daddy!" he screeched just as she set the mug on the table.

She turned around when Nate opened the back door. "You're just in time for hot cocoa."

His eyebrows rose when he looked at his son's mug. "Wow."

"'S got whipped cream, Daddy." Hayden stuck one finger into it, giggling.

"I see. Don't make a mess, buddy."

"And it's still hot, Hayden. Brownie first."

He pulled his brownie closer. "Okay." He took a big bite of his brownie.

Nate shook his head but turned his attention back to

Lucie. "Are you sure you don't mind?"

"Harry and Mindi said in case. I think this qualifies." She poured more of the dark liquid into the other mug and tipped it toward him.

He shook his head. "I think you need that more than I do. You're probably frozen from being outside all that time."

She wrapped her fingers around the mug. "A little." The heat of the cocoa seeped into the pottery, warming her fingertips. "You heard from your mom?"

"Yeah. The doctor was just in. They're running a couple more tests, and after that, barring anything unforeseen, he should get the all-clear to come home." Nate shifted his shoulders, as if trying to ease some tension.

Lucie moved around him and plucked the keys from the rack inside the door. "I'm sure he'll pass the tests with flying colors." She held the key ring out to him as she retraced her steps.

He closed his fingers on hers, and heat jolted up her arm. Her gaze flew to his face, noting the glint in his eyes. "Thank you, Lucie," he said softly.

She blushed. "It's no problem."

He snagged her mug and took a quick sip. "Where's your whipped cream?" He handed the cocoa back.

"I couldn't wait."

"That's really good." He released her hand.

"Best hot choc'late ever, Daddy!" Hayden shouted.

"You think everything is the best ever," she teased.

"Only when you make it."

She smiled at the whipped cream on the tip of his nose and glanced up at Nate, who shook his head again.

"All right, then I'll head to the hospital."

"You can get to the garage through there." She pointed to the door at the end of the hall, near the powder room. "Oh, wait! I have a casserole for you to take along, though." She stepped away, sliding the cooled casserole into the travel pack. "So your mom doesn't have to worry about dinner tonight. And some brownies for dessert." She added the brownies she'd wrapped up earlier, then held it out to Nate.

He hesitated for a second, then took the bag. "Thank you, Lucie. Mom will appreciate that."

She shrugged. "It was nothing."

He opened his mouth, then closed it for a second. "I'll see you guys later."

"Bye, Daddy," Hayden said around a mouthful of brownie.

Lucie set her mug on the table. "You've got whipped cream on your nose, buddy." She watched Nate close the garage door behind him, then wiped off Hayden's messy face. "You sure were hungry, weren't you? I hope you saved room for lunch."

The garage door rumbled up, and the engine started.

"What's for lunch?"

She smiled. "We'll figure that out in a little while, okay?"

———

WHILE HAYDEN NAPPED, SHE PUT DINNER TOGETHER AND into the oven. It would be some time before he woke, she realized, glancing at the clock. She dug out her laptop and set it up at the kitchen table. Might as well tweak her résumé while he was sleeping. It couldn't hurt to start her job search for real.

She tinkered with the résumé for a bit, but there wasn't much left to change since she'd spent so much time on it already. Taking a deep breath, she opened one of the job search sites and uploaded the document. Then again and once more. When she'd finished, her stomach had twisted into knots.

She pushed to her feet and went to the counter where she'd left her water glass. The sky outside the window churned heavy dark clouds past the bluff. She hoped the rain held off until Nate got his parents home. Maneuvering his father's wheelchair into the house might be challenging enough when the ramp was dry, even with his strength.

She leaned on the counter. Last night... Wow.

Quite a drought-ender.

She fanned herself when her cheeks warmed. The man could kiss. Among other things.

Her phone buzzed, startling her, and she jumped, then reached over to pick it up. Nate. She thumbed it on. "Hi."

"Hi. I'm just leaving Mom and Dad's. The van was perfect, thank you."

She smiled. "You're welcome."

"And Mom says thanks so much for dinner. The first thing she said when I got to the hospital was that we'd have to stop on the way home to pick something up because she's too tired to cook. That was really thoughtful, Lucie."

"It was nothing."

"Is it naptime?"

She chuckled. "Yes. I was thinking I might wake him up soon. He didn't want to sleep, so it took a while to get him to lie down, and then he passed right out. But I don't want him to sleep too long now and not sleep tonight for you."

He was silent for a few moments. "That's probably a good idea," he said finally. "What are you working on?"

"Oh, um, dinner's in the oven, and I just made my fingers stop shaking long enough to hit 'upload' on a couple of job search sites to post my résumé." Her stomach tightened again.

"Ah. Moving past denial, I see."

She smiled. "I guess. No, not really. Just trying to be realistic. I don't think Harry and Mindi are going to want a squatter when they come home." Her smile faded. God, she hoped she had a job by the time they returned.

Nate cleared his throat. "Well, I'll see you in a few minutes."

"Okay."

When he disconnected, she glanced over her shoulder at her laptop. She really had to have a job waiting when her friends came home. How depressing it would be to have nothing.

She bit her lip. She'd just have to make sure she did.

———

WHEN HE STEPPED INTO THE KITCHEN FROM THE GARAGE, A somber Lucie sat at the table, her laptop in front of her. Nate closed the door behind him. She smiled, though it was rather half-hearted. He realized she was more worried about the job search than she wanted to admit. He hung the SUV keys beside the back door again, trying to think of something to cheer her up.

"Have you thought about the restaurant?" he heard himself say as he unzipped his coat.

For a long moment, she was silent, staring down at her hands on the table. "What if I stayed on the island? This is supposed to be temporary. All of it." She pushed to her feet and crossed to the oven, bending to look inside it.

Temporary. Yes, it was supposed to be temporary. What if she did stay? He wasn't looking for a relationship. Neither was she. Nate shrugged. "That's up to you," he said finally. He had to admit, though, he kind of liked the idea of her sticking around. Way more than he should.

Lucie straightened. "I could meet with him, but I really doubt I can make a go of it. I don't know the first thing about running a restaurant."

"You know how to cook."

She shut her mouth into a flat line and leveled a narrow-eyed look at him that reminded him of Hayden when he'd been out-maneuvered. He bit back a smile.

Finally, she exhaled roughly. "That's a pretty small part of running a business, Nate. So I can cook. I don't know anything at all about book-keeping or licensing, or who knows what else there is to running a restaurant."

"Then you learn what you can, and hire someone who knows the rest."

"You make this sound so easy."

"I run a business, and I don't do everything myself."

She frowned. "Really?"

He shook his head. "I don't have time to do it all. I used to do it all, but after a few years, there was too much work and not enough time to do the other necessary things. So now I do all my own scheduling, all the actual work, but I have an accountant who takes care of the money things for me. He does the taxes, deals with all of those forms and numbers, so I can design and build. Mom and Dad help with Hayden, and Mom deals with marketing." He shrugged. "I couldn't do everything without help. No one can. So you get help for the parts you can't manage or don't want to manage."

She bit her lower lip and looked away for a moment. "I'll think about it." Her ungracious tone suggested the opposite.

Nate decided to leave well enough alone. "Supper smells good. You keep feeding us. You should really let me make dinner one night."

She smiled. "In your spare time?"

He narrowed his own eyes.

"Besides, I like cooking. It's been a while since I had anyone to cook for." Her wistful tone made him smile.

She wanted the restaurant. She just hadn't admitted it to herself yet.

She pushed away from the counter. "I should wake Hayden so he'll sleep for you later."

Nate shoved to his feet, chair scraping against the floor, and she froze, mid-step. *Good instincts.* He crossed to where she stood and cupped her face in his hands. Her eyes darkened, and he heard her swallow. "I've been thinking about this since last night when you left," he whispered, bending to brush a kiss on her mouth.

Her lips parted a little, so he went back for another. A faint taste of chocolate when he slipped his tongue over hers. He smiled against her mouth, then lifted his head. "You taste like hot chocolate, Lucie."

She laughed, her chin dipping. "I had more after Hayden fell asleep. Liquid courage for the job search."

Nate nudged her nose with his own, and her smile faded. Her hands slid up his chest to his shoulders, then wrapped around his nape. Warm. He dropped one of his hands to her hip, giving a light squeeze.

She sucked in a quick breath, and he caught her mouth, for real this time.

He hadn't imagined it. The pleasure arcing through him, the easy way she responded.

He hauled her closer. Her short nails dug into his nape, and she pressed nearer. He felt her hard little nipples through her sweater, and he dragged his hand up from her hip, under the hem of the heavy top. Bare skin. Warm. He cupped her breast through thin satin and stroked his thumb cross the tip. "Feel so good," he muttered.

Lucie arched into the next stroke, and he lifted her onto

the counter beside them, still kissing her. Her thighs settled around his waist. He rocked into her. He shouldn't be so hard so soon.

She tightened her legs around him, keeping him pressed into her. "We shouldn't," she muttered against his mouth. As her fingers tugged his shirt up so she could reach skin.

Couldn't, he realized. "Shit." He lifted his head a few inches. "I didn't replace the condom in my wallet."

Her warm fingers flattened against his ribs, and she caught her lower lip in her teeth for a second. Her breath came too fast. "That's too bad," she managed after a moment, her dark eyes locked on his face. "But maybe for the best."

He scowled down at her, hauling her tighter to him so her lashes fluttered down. "Really?"

A faint smile curved her swollen lips. "We do need to wake Hayden, and then it'll be supper time."

"And you're going to come over afterward."

She pulled in a ragged breath. "That wasn't a question."

He shook his head.

One of her eyebrows lifted.

His fingers tightened on her, ass and breast, and her breath snagged again.

"Okay," she whispered.

He groaned and caught her mouth once more. He knew how to be a responsible adult. He'd been doing it for a long time, but fuck it, he wanted her right now. He didn't want to wait interminable hours.

She stretched up, pressing closer for a moment, then pulled back, eyes squeezed shut. "You're too tempting." The words warmed his mouth. "You make me forget all the reasons we shouldn't."

Nate growled. "And what are they?"

"I don't remember." Her eyes opened, and she smiled,

easing her hand from under his shirt so she could stroke his jaw. "You taste good, too."

He squeezed his own eyes shut against the rush of pleasure at her words.

"Let go, Nate." She patted his cheek.

He didn't want to. Instead, he lifted her off the counter, smiling at her yelp, and carried her into the living room. He dropped onto the sofa and settled her on his lap. "Give me a minute."

She didn't argue. Just put her head against his shoulder and took a deep breath.

He inhaled slowly, too, trying to redirect his thoughts away from his dick. "I didn't ask what you made for supper."

"I have a roast and vegetables in the oven." Her fingers rubbed against his chest.

"Smells good." He put his face in her hair. She smelled good, too. That wasn't helping. He was still hard against her hip. Stifling a groan, he straightened. "What are you doing this weekend?"

"Taking a quick drive off-island to pick up mail, restock the pantry. Spend as little time with strangers as possible."

He smiled. "You're starting to sound like a native."

She shook her head. "It just seems like a lot after being by myself for a few weeks."

He realized he'd never asked how long she was staying. Usually Harry and Mindi's trips were a couple of months long, but they'd left early this year.

"I shouldn't get too used to solitude. Once I have to re-enter the real world, it won't be like this."

He frowned.

Lucie tipped her head back, and he made his frown go away. "Is Nate short for something?"

He blinked. "Nathaniel. My grandfather's name."

She smiled slightly.

"What about Lucie?"

Her smile twisted. "Lucrezia."

"As in Borgia?" He grinned.

She laughed. "Well, it's spelled the same, but I'm named after one of my grandmother's cousins."

"Interesting."

She shook her head. "Just another old family name, like Nathaniel. But Lucrezia is a lot for a toddler to be able to say, so I became Lucie a long time ago."

He brushed a strand of hair away from her cheek, trying to imagine her as a little girl with a big name.

She stretched up and kissed him quickly. "I need to empty the dishwasher, and we need to wake Hayden up. Dinner will be ready in an hour or so."

He let her go this time, watching the sway of her hips as she strode to the kitchen. Blowing out a slow breath, he shoved to his feet and turned in the opposite direction.

He found Hayden sprawled in the middle of one of the beds, his blond hair sticking up on one side. He smiled and sat on the edge of the bed. "Hey, buddy," he said softly, stroking one chubby cheek.

The little boy didn't flinch.

"Hayden, it's time to get up." He pitched this a little louder.

Still nothing.

He shook his head, smile widening. "Buddy, it's almost time for supper." He jostled the bed.

His son shifted, frowning, one small hand curling into a fist.

"I think I might eat the rest of the brownies," he continued, giving the mattress another shake.

Hayden's frown turned to a scowl, and his blue eyes opened to slits. "No."

Nate chuckled. "Still sleepy, buddy?"

He nodded.

"You must have played pretty hard today."

His son smiled. "I like playin' with Lucie. She's fun." He rubbed a fist against his eye. "An' she makes good stuff to eat."

"That she does. Supper smells pretty good right now."

"I helped." Hayden rolled onto his side to face him. "I cleaned carrots an' potatoes."

"Good job." He smoothed down the boy's hair. "We should probably help Lucie and set the table since she keeps cooking for us."

"'Kay." Hayden sat up and yawned. "Is Grampa home?"

"He is. He's resting, and so is Grandma."

"Can we see 'im tomorrow?"

"I think he'd like that." Nate knew that would be both good and bad, since his dad was accustomed to being able to keep up with Hayden, but he was also accustomed to seeing him daily, so that would probably balance out the fact that he had to keep weight off of his injured leg until the doctor gave the all-clear. He pulled the blankets back. "Let's go help Lucie."

Hayden scrambled out of the bed. "I'll race you, Daddy!" He ran out of the room, not even waiting for his shoes, which Nate scooped up after he'd pulled the blankets back up to the pillow. He turned for the door and saw Lucie's green sweater hanging in the open closet. Lucie's room. He swallowed and forced his gaze to the hallway door instead.

Later. He could think about that later.

Chapter Eight

Lucie shivered when they opened the back door later to trek across the back yard.

"I think it's going to snow tonight." Nate glanced over his shoulder at her. "Did Harry show you where the shovels are? How to use his snow-blower? I don't think you should need that yet, but probably the shovel."

She pulled the door shut and followed him down the steps. "Yes, he did." It did feel like snow. The chilly air from earlier in the day had shifted to downright frigid since she and Hayden had been outside. She shivered inside her coat. "I was just hoping not to need them yet."

Nate unlocked his back door and set Hayden down, then stood aside so Lucie could precede him into the mud room. When the door closed behind them, Hayden was already hurrying upstairs. "Slow down on the steps, buddy!"

She unbuttoned her jacket and turned to hang it on one of the pegs, and Nate caught her hand when she'd finished. She flushed at the expression in his eyes. "Behave," she whispered.

He leaned down and pressed a quick kiss on her mouth. "We'll see." He released her and headed into the kitchen.

She followed, more slowly. She needed to think about something else. Something besides what they'd started earlier.

Hayden was halfway down the steps when she got to the living room, his bear and a book in his hands. "I wanna read, Daddy."

"Already?"

The little boy nodded. "I'm tired."

Nate sat on the sofa and patted his knee. "Climb on up." He glanced up at Lucie and winked.

She looked away, face heating, and sank onto the chair nearest to the fireplace. It was oversized and cushy. She relaxed. It would be pretty close to perfect if the fire was going and she had a book of her own to read. Maybe a glass of wine. She exhaled slowly, more tension easing out of her muscles.

Nate read to his son, whose eyes drooped, fluttering shut more than once before they got to the last story. "And they lived happily ever after," he read at last, closing the book. He looked down at his son, who snuggled close. "Let's get you tucked in, buddy."

"'Kay, Daddy," he murmured. "Night, Lucie."

She watched Nate rise, hefting his sleepy son on one arm, and head up the steps. She should be keeping her distance, from both of them. She'd only be here for a couple of months, and then she'd go back to her real world.

She pushed to her feet, thinking about the résumés she'd sent earlier. None of the postings were for anything she'd been excited about, but she was starting to feel like she had to find something. Or at least make an effort to find something.

She walked to the dark fireplace and rested one hand on the cool stone mantle.

She needed to not panic. Not yet. She'd only just started searching.

Soft footfalls on the steps alerted her to Nate's return, and she glanced over her shoulder as he came down the last few stairs.

"Hey." His mouth hitched up a little at one side. "You okay?"

"Just thinking about jobs." She shrugged. "I don't want to think about it now."

He crossed the floor to her. "I might be able to help with that."

She smiled as he caught her arm to turn her in his direction. "Really?"

"Yeah, I think we left something unfinished earlier." He pulled her flush against him.

Lucie sucked in a quick breath at the hard muscles pressed against her. Just like earlier. Need flared to life all over. She slid her hands up to his shoulders. "Did we?" she whispered.

He nudged his knee between her thighs, and her breath rushed out. "Oh, yeah." He caught her hips and lifted a little so his growing erection notched against her.

"Hm, I'm starting to remember."

A fleeting smile crossed his lips before he captured her mouth roughly. She wrapped one arm around his neck, and both legs around his waist. He groaned into the kiss, his fingers digging into her ass as he dragged her along the length of his cock.

Heat blasted her face, her belly. "Oh God," she muttered against his mouth, trying to get closer to him.

Nate nipped at her mouth, pressing her tighter to him.

"We need a bed this time, Lucie. I have a nice big bed upstairs."

His hard fingers sliding down to stroke her stole all thought right out of her head. Pleasure made her light-headed.

"Say yes, Lucie." He kissed her again, deep and wet. "Say yes."

"Yes." If he kept doing *that*, she'd agree to anything. She just wanted more.

Nate turned, but she barely noticed, she was so focused on his fingers rubbing between her legs, over her clit, making her wetter, needier. She kissed his jaw, his stubbled chin, his throat.

And when he carried her down beneath him onto his bed, she bit her lip against a moan.

He pushed up onto his elbows, and she wanted to protest. She wanted his full weight over her. But he stroked her hair away from her forehead, his eyes dark with need. The same need that commanded her. A faint smile curved his mouth. "I want to take my time with you, Lucie, but I don't think I can this first time."

First time.

Her pulse tripped at his words. She tightened her legs around his waist and rolled her hips to grind against his erection.

His smile vanished, and he yanked the hem of her sweater up, past her breasts, so the cooler air in the room washed over her skin. She had to let go of him so he could pull the garment off over her head. Her nipples puckered even tighter. His gaze dropped to her bra, and he reached in between them with one hand to undo the clasp. Her breath rushed out as he tugged the lace and cotton aside, and then she gasped when he bent to scrape his teeth along one tight peak.

Desire slammed into her belly, white-hot. "Nate," she

whispered. She dragged one hand down to his hip, trying to pull him closer.

He obliged by rocking against her, pressure right over her clit so she trembled. Again. He sucked on her nipple so she arched into him, his mouth hot and demanding.

"I need...oh, God, Nate..."

He wrestled her jeans open and down, along with her panties, and then his hard fingers were there, slipping through the wet folds of her sex. "Oh, Lucie, you're killing me." He pressed two fingers inside her and thumbed her clit.

Release jolted through her at the hard strokes, and she swallowed back a cry.

"Fuck." His breath washed over her breast, and he lifted up onto his elbow, then pushed onto his knees, still stroking her clit. "I have to be inside you." He unfastened his jeans with his free hand, then leaned over to snag a condom from the night table, tearing it open with his teeth.

She tried to take in a deep breath, but he shifted so he could yank her pants off the rest of the way, then covered his erection with the condom before he shoved deep. The breath stuck in her chest as her hips lifted involuntarily, helping him settle as far inside her as possible.

Lucie couldn't think about anything, nothing but the feel of Nate all around her, inside her. The taste of him when he kissed her again, desperation and possession darkening the flavor. She met his tongue with her own, his hips with hers, feeling the impossible rise of her need again.

His pace was so fast, she didn't have time to think about the improbability of another orgasm before it rushed over her, left her shaking and spent. Before he groaned with his own release, his body taut and quaking above her. After a few moments, he collapsed to his elbows, then rolled onto his side, keeping her close. "Just a minute," he panted against her forehead.

She couldn't answer. She had no breath, and no functioning brain cells to formulate a response.

———

Nate stroked Lucie's damp hair away from her temple when he returned to the bed. Her dark lashes lifted, and a gentle smile curved her lips. He slid in beside her, gathering her closer. Warm. Better.

She let out a slow breath against his chest. "Wow."

He grinned, then realized he probably looked very smug. He tried to erase the grin, but couldn't quite manage it. "You okay?"

She chuckled. "I think okay might be an understatement." Her soft fingers stroked up his spine. "That was pretty spectacular, actually."

He laughed then, he couldn't help it. He turned his face into the pillow to try to muffle the sound, and Lucie giggled into his chest.

God, this felt good. Not just the warm, naked woman tucked against him, but all of it. The ease of them together, laughing in the dark, was new. He couldn't remember that with Greta. Then again, it had been so long since they were together, he barely remembered any of it, even the good.

He settled more comfortably under the blankets, and Lucie let out a slow breath, relaxing still more.

"I should go before I get any sleepier," she murmured.

His fingers tightened on her involuntarily. "Not already."

He felt her smile against his skin. "Well, we did only use one of your stash of condoms, didn't we?"

He chuckled. "Yeah, we have to use at least one more before we can call it a night."

Her fingers slid lower, gliding over his ass. "Well, since you insist..." Warmth followed her touch around his hip to his thigh.

Suddenly he wasn't relaxed anymore.

She brushed her fingers down the side of his leg, lightly, then back up.

Inches away, his dick came to attention.

"Mm." She stroked one fingertip over the sensitive tip, and he clenched his jaw at the rush of pleasure. "You feel good, Nate," she whispered, wrapping her fingers around his shaft.

"What you're doing feels pretty damn good." He squeezed his eyes shut when her grip tightened.

"Good." Her warm breath skimmed along his chest a second before her tongue slid over his nipple.

Fuck. His fingers clenched on her ass. Pleasure roared through him again, straight from the stroke of her tongue to his cock, growing harder in her hand.

He wanted to protest when she sat up, but in the next instant, she'd shoved the blankets away and her lips stroked over the head of his erection.

Double fuck. He swallowed back a groan.

Her mouth was heaven. Wet and hot, teasing licks and kisses, serious sucks. Her fingers stroked over him, too, grazing his balls, his thigh, the base of his cock when she couldn't take all of it into her mouth.

He didn't know how long he let her have her way, but he knew when he'd reached his limit. He sat up and caught her by the waist, flipping her onto her back in the middle of the bed. She stifled a cry with one hand. He pushed her knees apart and bent to nudge her hand away from her mouth, just long enough for a hard kiss. Then he retreated so he could bend to her sex.

Her gasp made him smile, fleetingly, before he licked over her swollen little clit.

Her hips jolted up, and he set one hand low on her belly to hold her down where he wanted her.

She was already wet when he slipped his fingers over her. Aroused enough for him to slide deep and sate them both again.

But he wanted to taste her orgasm this time.

He nibbled at her clit, licked around it, inside her. Her hips lifted to meet him, but he pressed her flat on the bed again. Then thrust two fingers inside her as he sucked on her clit.

Her broken moan drifted to his ears, but he was too busy enjoying the taste of her, the slick, tight muscles clenching on his fingers. When he pressed one more finger into her, he scraped his teeth carefully along her swollen little clit, and her release burst free.

She muffled a wail in one of the pillows, her entire body quaking with the orgasm. He stroked his tongue over her, lifting his gaze to study her, the flush that reached from her tight, puckered nipples to the roots of her hair, the sheen of perspiration on her skin.

"So pretty." He didn't realize he'd said it aloud until she moved the pillow away from her mouth and smiled.

"Thank you," she managed, breathless.

He kissed the inside of her thigh and shifted up over her again, reaching for a condom. Her warm gaze followed his movements, making him more aware of the need pulsing through him, all settled in his dick. Holding her gaze, he nudged the tip of his sheathed erection along her clit. She shuddered.

"Please, Nate." She didn't look away.

"Turn over." He didn't know what made him say it, not when he wanted nothing more than to be balls-deep inside her. But her flush deepened, and she shifted to obey him. He caught her hips and lifted her onto her knees, planting his own between them. "Oh, Lucie," he whispered, stroking one finger down over the curve of her ass to the swollen folds between her legs.

She shivered. "Nate."

He eased inside her, slowly. "Fuck."

She whimpered, trying to lift toward him, but he kept her still with his grip on her hips.

If he shoved deep now, it wouldn't take long before he lost control, and he wanted this to last longer than a few minutes.

He rocked back, so just the tip of his erection was still lodged inside her, and counted to ten. His heartbeat thundered against his ribs in a ragged rhythm. He inched into her again, just a little and felt the way her inner muscles tightened. He eased back once more, listening to her whimper.

"Please, please."

Do it, do it, do it. His pulse hammered in his head along with her pleas.

One of her hands landed on the side of his leg. "Nate."

He rocked deep and held still, a feat that took every bit of his self-control, resisting the siren call of her hot, tight sex.

Her short nails bit into his thigh.

He took a slow breath and withdrew, loving her whimpered protest. Eased in once more, just a few inches.

"God," she moaned, "Nate, you're killing me."

He grinned and shoved inside her.

Her body tightened.

Already. He released her hip and planted his hands beside

her head. "You're ruining my good intentions, Lucie." He kissed the top of her ear. "I wanted to take my time. Slow and easy." He gave a lazy thrust, pleased when she rocked back to meet him. "Touch yourself, Lucie."

Her breath caught, and after a few seconds, she released his leg. He felt her fingers brush his cock when she stroked her clit.

"Yes, just like that." He rocked against her. Slick, hot muscles rippled around him. God, that felt good.

Her breath snagged again, and she quickened her pace, the strokes of her clit and her rocking under him.

Nate didn't argue this time, pleasure burning hotter in his gut, sinking lower to settle in his groin. He matched her pace, nuzzling her hair aside to taste the warm skin on the side of her neck.

The release this time was less urgent, but no less massive, no less potent. Lucie buried her face in the pillow as she cried out, and he ground his teeth together to contain his own groan. Incredible. It was the last thing he could think when he rolled them to their sides.

―――――

Lucie startled awake when the warmth at her back disappeared.

"Shh." Nate stroked her shoulder. "I just need to get rid of this."

She took an unsteady breath and tried to focus. She was still at Nate's. Round two had been just as shattering as round one. More, maybe. She smiled, briefly, and then rolled onto her back. She needed to get to her own bed.

It didn't sound very appealing.

Which meant she needed to go now.

She pushed up onto one elbow and reached for the night table beside the bed, carefully searching for the small lamp. There.

She had to close her eyes for a moment against the glare.

"Are you okay?"

She flushed and opened her eyes again. "I'll never find my clothes in the dark," she said, forcing a little smile.

Nate's serious gaze didn't lighten.

She dragged her gaze away, and looked around her side of the bed. Her sweater and jeans lay there, and she could just see her panties at the foot of the bed. No bra. She blushed and took a slow breath.

"Missing something?"

She looked over and saw her bra dangling from one of his long fingers. More heat burned her cheeks.

He grinned.

"Thanks," she managed, reaching out to take it.

He planted one knee on the bed and leaned over to kiss her. "Are you sure you have to go?"

"Yes, I'm sure." She reached up to stroke his jaw. "I'd rather stay, but I really can't be here when Hayden gets up. I don't want to confuse him." Or herself.

Nate growled and turned his head slightly to nip at her palm. "I know. But–"

She covered his mouth with her hand and smiled again. "Can I use the bathroom?"

He nodded, then pressed a kiss on her hand. "I get it." He sighed and sat down.

She moved away, grabbing the rest of her clothing and rounding the foot of the bed to dash into his bathroom, and felt his gaze on her back the whole way. Her reflection in the mirror over the sink made her pink cheeks redden still more.

Tumbled hair, puffy lips, a faint bite mark on her neck. *Holy shit.*

She turned away from the mirror to pull on her clothes, then dragged her fingers through her messy hair until it resembled something like normal. She faced the mirror again.

Better. She took a deep breath and pulled the door open.

Nate had pulled on his jeans, though the button at his waist remained undone, drawing her gaze to the hard ridges of his abs.

Her mouth watered.

"If you keep looking at me like that, Lucie, you're never leaving tonight," he said, his tone a gravely rumble that went right to her belly.

She blushed and dragged her gaze to the faint grin tugging at his mouth. "Sorry."

He shook his head. "You don't have to be sorry. I was looking at you the same way when you hurried into the bathroom." He winked.

She laughed, softly. "You're a bad influence." She crossed the floor and leaned in to brush a soft kiss on his mouth. "I have to go."

"You keep saying that."

She straightened. "Because it's true." She patted his cheek. "Get some sleep."

One of his hands slid around her back before she could step away. "I called Stu's office on my way to the hospital earlier and made an appointment for you to meet him tomorrow to look at the restaurant."

Her mouth dropped open. "What?" Her heartbeat quickened.

He pushed to his feet, keeping his arm around her. "Two-thirty. It's two blocks from the ferry terminal. You can't miss it."

"You..." She closed her mouth and swallowed. "Why did you do that?" Panic started to seep into her veins.

"You needed a nudge. Just as another option."

She stared up at him. "But...Nate, I...I don't...I don't even know what to say to you right now."

A faint smile curved his mouth again. "You can say 'Nate, I'll be happy to watch Hayden in the morning for a couple of hours, and then, yes, I'll go meet Stu.' That's all."

She swallowed again, her heart beating faster, too fast. Panic rushed through her. "You know I'll watch Hayden."

"And?"

She bit her lip, then shook her head. "I...I don't know."

His eyes narrowed. "You can sleep on it, but you should do it. At least to rule out the possibility."

This was supposed to be temporary. The words were on the tip of her tongue.

He leaned down and brushed a soft kiss on her mouth. "If you're really set on not staying tonight, I'll walk you down," he whispered against her lips. He kissed her once more, then turned her toward the closed door.

Lucie let him, linking fingers as they walked down the steps to the living room, through the kitchen to the mud room. She concentrated on breathing evenly, on not thinking about what he'd done. He helped her into her coat, then threaded his fingers through her hair to kiss her. Slow, deep, lingering. Until she wanted to take off her clothes and go back upstairs with him.

Then he lifted his head and stroked her cheek. "You have your key?"

She put her hand into her pocket and closed her fingers on the key fob. "Yes."

"I'll see you in the morning. You sure you don't mind keeping him?"

She smiled. "I don't mind. Are you going to your parents'?"

"I thought I'd get a little work done first, and then take him over in the afternoon."

Convenient. She narrowed her eyes at him, but he just grinned.

"Sleep well, Lucie." He kissed her again, briefly this time.

She took a shaky breath. "You, too." She stepped away and reached for the door knob.

The light over the back door shone brightly, so brightly she could see tiny snowflakes blowing in from the yard. It was a good distraction.

"Snow." She smiled. "I'll see you guys in the morning." She tugged the door open and stepped out into the cold wind. "Holy shit." She bundled her coat collar up around her neck and hurried across the yard, through the gate and up her own back steps.

Inside, she shed her coat and locked the door. She'd worry about getting the shovel out in the morning. The snow was so light she might only need a broom.

And she would *not* think about tomorrow afternoon. Not now.

Chapter Nine

Nate couldn't tell what Lucie was thinking. He'd dropped Hayden off a couple of hours ago, and she'd greeted them with her usual morning cheer, but no mention of her afternoon plans. He finished assembling a cabinet frame and paused to brush a fleck of sawdust from under his eye. He hoped she'd go meet Stu.

And that she wasn't pissed at him for arranging it without asking her.

He blew out a hard breath and glanced over to where his phone vibrated on the work table. His mom. "Hi."

"Am I interrupting, Nate?"

"Of course not. I just finished the last cabinet frame for the Holder job. What's going on?"

"Oh, nothing. We're fine. I just wondered if you might bring Hayden over later. I think he might cheer your dad up."

He smiled. "I actually planned to do that this afternoon. I wanted to get some of this framing out of the way first."

"Thank you. I know your dad would love to see him. I've got some soup on, so maybe for lunch?"

Nate winced. He'd have to let Lucie know. "Yeah, I think

we can probably do that. Then I can put Hayden down for a nap when it's time."

"Great, then we'll see you two a little later."

"Yeah, sure, Mom."

He exhaled roughly. Text or in person? Maybe text for this one, he thought. He pulled up her number and thought for a minute.

"Mom just called & asked if I'd bring Hayden 4 lunch today. I told her I would so he can see Dad. That means you have time to get ready for your meeting with Stu." He pushed send.

It took twenty minutes for her to reply. He counted every single one of them.

"Okay."

"Shit." He scowled at the screen. She was angry.

He put down the handful of screws he held and paced away from the cabinet. It had been impulsive, he thought, calling Stu's office yesterday. High-handed, maybe.

He blew out a hard breath, looking at the flurries flying outside. He should've asked her before doing it. Or just left it alone. He'd already made the suggestion. She was an adult, fully capable of deciding what she did and didn't want to do.

He braced one hand against the window frame and leaned in to press his forehead against the cool glass. He'd screw this up if he wasn't careful.

That made him frown.

What was there to screw up? A temporary-neighbors-with-benefits situation?

But he liked Lucie.

And that was the problem.

Shit.

He yanked the door open and strode across the yard to the

gate. When he stepped up to her back door, he banged on it once.

Her wide eyes turned wary when she peered around the edge of the curtain, and, after a second, she pulled the door open, letting a rush of heat and the scent of cinnamon out.

"Look, I'm sorry I took the decision out of your hands, Lucie."

She blinked, then looked away for a moment. "You know it's snowing, right? And you aren't wearing a coat."

He frowned as she stepped back, opening the door wider, but he went inside, pushing the door shut behind him. "Did you hear what I said?"

She blushed faintly. "I did." She glanced over her shoulder to where Hayden sat at the coffee table in the living room with a coloring book and crayons, not paying them any attention.

"You don't have to go. I'll call and tell them you can't make it."

She reached up with one hand and covered his mouth. "I'll go," she said softly.

His brain couldn't decide on the most important thing just now–her warm, soft hand on his mouth, or her agreeing to look at the restaurant. He caught her wrist and brushed a kiss on her palm as he pulled her fingers away from his face. "Thank you." He bent and kissed her.

Just briefly, but it still made him want to kiss her again, for real.

Except Hayden was looking at them curiously when he straightened. *Hell.*

His son returned to his coloring after a second, evidently deciding it wasn't anything too interesting.

Lucie's blush deepened so her cheeks were bright pink, and her wide eyes filled with alarm.

Nate smiled, restraining the urge to laugh at the two of them. "It's fine," he whispered.

She shot a quick glance into the living room, then met his gaze again, a shallow frown line between her brows.

"I've got to go finish this cabinet, and then I'll be back for Hayden in about half an hour, okay?"

She nodded once. "Sounds good."

Without waiting for more, he headed back outside, suddenly realizing how cold it was. The snow flurries were bigger now, too, he noticed as he jogged back to his workshop. He should take the shovel to the house with him when he finished. In case it turned into more than just snow showers.

He smiled as he closed the door to the shop. She was going to look at the restaurant.

He shouldn't be so happy about that. What if she stayed?

His smile didn't abate, but spread.

Holy shit.

———

Bat-sized butterflies crowded Lucie's stomach as she drove into town. She must have lost her mind when she agreed to meet Stu. She couldn't possibly run a restaurant. All she was good at was cooking. And teaching people to sell electronics.

Her fingers tightened on the steering wheel. But her teenage self had wanted to be a cook. To have her own restaurant.

She took a slow breath. She should be practical. Her parents had talked her into practicality a long time ago.

She'd be practical. But she would at least do the walk-through with Stu. Then she could say 'no, thank you', and go back to her search for a real, practical job.

There.

Her breath caught. The long, low building hugged the harbor, weathered wood siding accented with dark green shutters at the front windows and trim the same color framing the door, where a tall, thin man with faded red hair waited under the porch roof. She eased her car into a spot close to his expensive sedan and inhaled carefully. She could do this. Quick, polite, and get out.

Still, her fingers trembled when she took the key from the ignition and stepped out of her car.

"You must be Lucie." The man smiled and approached, his right hand out. "I'm Stu, Nate's uncle."

Uncle? "It's nice to meet you, Stu. I'm Lucie Russo." She shook his hand.

"Let's get in out of this snow, all right?" He led the way to the door and pulled it open. "I came a little early to turn up the heat and get all the lights on." He held the door for her.

She swallowed hard and stepped inside. "Oh."

Oh, damn.

The entire opposite wall was windows that looked out over the harbor.

I hate you, Nate, she thought, walking further inside, past the neat, rustic host station, threading between tables to the other wall.

A new deck stretched from the wall of the restaurant toward the water's edge. She imagined tables there topped with umbrellas, maybe green and white, rather than the dusting of light snow it wore now.

"Ah, the deck. They just redid that in the spring. The tables and umbrellas are in storage for the winter," Stu said from behind her.

Of course they were. "What color are the umbrellas?" She didn't know why she asked.

"Dark green like the trim around the door and windows, with white stripes." He stopped beside her. "It is a nice view, even in the winter, isn't it? This is the first year they haven't been open year-round."

Lucie swallowed. "What kind of hours did they have over the winter? I wouldn't think it would be as busy, without the summer tourists."

"It wasn't, but they opened for lunch and dinner Tuesday through Saturday for the locals. It's just, well, this year, the owner had a heart attack, and he can't do it anymore." Stu looked regretful. "And Jenny, his wife, doesn't want to run it by herself. It was really his baby. No one else on the island is interested in it."

Uh-oh. She made her lips curve into a polite smile. "Is the kitchen that way?" She pointed toward a closed door to her left.

"No, that's the private party room. They rented it out for events...birthdays, showers, that kind of thing. Come and see."

She half-listened while he talked about how many people the smaller room accommodated, how many people the entire restaurant accommodated, what the traffic was like in different seasons. But her mind raced far ahead, thinking about menus and help, and, oh God, she shouldn't go there.

When they stepped into the kitchen, her heart leaped into overdrive. Her dream kitchen. Times ten. *"Oh!"*

Stu stopped talking behind her, and she took a moment to look around. Several big stoves and ovens, so much prep space, walk-in freezers and refrigerators. A tidy little desk area tucked into the farthest corner.

Her chest hurt. She *wanted* this. As much as she'd wanted

it at fifteen. *More*, now that it was right here, and she could touch it. She realized she was stroking a cool metal work table as she walked by it. That didn't stop her, though, from touching anything else as she moved through the big room.

"Nate didn't ask the office about numbers when he called. I should probably mention those while we're here," Stu said after she'd circled the entire kitchen.

Her heart sank. Back to reality.

"They really want the restaurant to find a good owner, so they're offering a very generous owner-financing to the buyer."

She bit her lip. "What is the asking price?" She would have to summon up her polite face, make more polite conversation for a few minutes, tell him she'd have to consider, blah-blah.

He hesitated, then named the figure.

Lucie's head buzzed. That wasn't out of the realm of possibility. Her pulse skipped several beats. She had her settlement from the company move, plus the money she'd saved...

"You're smiling."

She blinked. "Am I?" She realized she was. "I didn't...well, I have to think about this. It's a big decision."

"But it isn't out of the question." The older man smiled, too.

"No, it isn't. I must be insane," she added in a mutter.

His smile widened. "Then you'll fit right in on the island." He produced a business card from his pocket. "Why don't you think about it, and then you can call me when you feel like you're ready to talk about more than abstracts. Maybe in a week or so."

She took the card and studied the crisp white rectangle with a blur of black text. "That sounds good," she murmured.

The rational part of her brain would be back in control by then, and it could be a short conversation.

She slid into her car a minute later and took a shaky breath. She knew she couldn't pull this off. But that didn't make her want it any less. She took one last look and started the car. She could go back to the house and start making a list of all the reasons why it would never work.

And it would be a really, really long list.

———

Nate eased the truck into his driveway later and realized he hadn't left any lights on. In the dusk, light shone from Lucie's kitchen window, though.

He wondered if she'd gone to look at the restaurant or chickened out.

"Daddy, wave to Mr. Micah."

He glanced up at the lighthouse, where the shadow stood at one of the windows, and waved to placate his son.

"Are we gonna go see Lucie? I wanna show her my pi'ture."

He considered that as he took his keys from the ignition. "Maybe we should invite Lucie for supper at our house tonight. She keeps making supper for us."

"Yeah!"

Nate winced at the volume of his son's agreement. "Okay, hang on, I'll come get you."

In under a minute, he stepped up to her back door and knocked, more politely than he had that morning, hefting Hayden on his arm.

It took a few moments for her to tug the edge of the curtain aside, and Hayden waved. She blinked, then smiled, pulling the door open. "Hi, guys."

"We came to ask you to eat with us," Hayden announced before they were inside.

Her eyes widened. "Is it really supper time?" She glanced away. "Crap," she muttered.

Nate pushed the door shut. "Not quite yet. Are we interrupting something?"

"No, I just lost track of the time."

He glanced around. The dining table was covered with papers, pens, high-lighters, two yellow legal pads, and her open laptop, which had a restaurant supply website on the screen. He bit back a smile and bent to set his son down. By the time he straightened, she'd closed the laptop and shoved everything else into a messy pile.

Cheeks pink, she met his gaze.

He'd wait and ask her later. "How do you feel about spaghetti and meatballs?"

She smiled again. "One of my favorites." She looked down at Hayden. "How about you?"

"Yes! I help make the meatballs!" The little boy jumped up and down a few times.

"Well, in that case, I would love to." She met Nate's gaze again. "I need to clean up, but I can get some garlic bread ready and bring wine."

He nodded. "That sounds great. Come over when you're ready."

"Come now!"

She blinked at Hayden's demand.

"You can make the bread in our house."

"He has a point. I don't need the oven or broiler for anything. Then we can open the wine earlier." Nate winked when she glanced up.

"Even better." She smoothed Hayden's hair down. "Okay, you twisted my arm, buddy."

"I didn't twist your arm." He frowned up at her.

Nate chuckled. "It means you talked her into it, Hayden."

"Oh." His son's frown vanished. "Come on, get your coat, Lucie."

"Yes, sir." She saluted him, then picked up the mug that sat on the table, carrying it to the sink to rinse. "Let me grab the bread and garlic, and I'll be right over."

"I'll wait for you." Hayden stuck his hands into his pockets.

"Then I'll go get the kitchen fired up," Nate said. "I'll see you two in a couple minutes." He headed outside, into the whirls of flurries still skittering down, and jogged across the yards.

After shedding his coat and boots, he set about defrosting some ground beef and turned on the broiler so it would be ready when Lucie needed it for garlic bread. By the time his son led Lucie into the house, he had the big pot of water on for the pasta, and the meat in a bowl so he could add the other ingredients.

Lucie looked more relaxed when Hayden dragged her into the kitchen by her free hand. His son carried a foil-wrapped loaf of bread tucked between his arm and his body, and Nate hoped he wasn't squashing it. In her other arm, Lucie had a bottle of wine and a head of garlic. She smiled at him when they neared the counter.

"I'm ready to help, Daddy!"

"Not until you wash your grubby hands, you're not." Nate held out his hand for the bread. His son handed it over, then ran to the half bath.

Lucie chuckled and set her own things on the island. "I should probably do the same before I start touching food. What do you put in the meatballs?" She went to the sink to wash up.

"Egg, bread crumbs, some spices." He hadn't realized...well, his meatballs might not be up to Lucie's standards.

"Sounds good." She smiled. "I need to roast the garlic before we can put it on the bread. Thanks for turning the broiler on already." When she stretched up to kiss his cheek, he froze. By the time he recovered his wits, she'd already moved away.

Hayden ran back to him, shouting that he was ready, so he set up at the table, where his son could reach everything. While they mixed up the meatballs, Lucie found the foil to wrap her garlic and put it into the oven and set the timer before moving on to taking dishes out for their meal. Nate dragged his gaze away so he could roll meatballs and put them onto a plate.

This was too comfortable. He shouldn't be enjoying it so much, this domestic scene with the three of them in the kitchen. Even if she somehow found the courage to stay and take on the restaurant, they were temporary. They were especially temporary if she didn't stay to take on the restaurant.

He shouldn't be getting comfortable. He shouldn't be letting Hayden get comfortable.

When she smiled at him from the sink, he smiled back, desire sliding along his veins.

It was just lust.

He relaxed. That 'new relationship' rush, when you couldn't keep your hands off one another. And then it went away, just like she probably would. He set the last meatball onto the plate and picked up the plate and bowl to carry to the sink.

He ignored the knot that lodged in his gut at the idea of her leaving. It didn't matter. He'd been alone with Hayden for a long time, and he expected they would be alone together a lot longer. Lucie was just a pleasant little break from that.

"Can I do anything?" she asked while he washed his hands.

"I'm going to open that wine in a minute, and then you should have some." He looked back over his shoulder and found her hovering near the island. "How long does the garlic need?"

"It'll take a little while, almost as long as your meatballs, I think."

"Then you definitely need the wine. And to sit." He reached for a towel and dried off. "It's our turn to make dinner." He rehung the towel and found the corkscrew.

"I've been sitting too long today," she said, stuffing her hands into her jeans pockets.

He opened the bottle, then carried it to the counter to get two glasses out. He poured some of the dark red liquid into each glass, then took one to her. "This smells good." It had been a while since he had any wine.

She smiled. "It's just your basic red, goes with almost every Italian dish you can think of." She took the glass.

"Lucie, come look at my picture!"

Nate chuckled. "He wanted to show that to you earlier, and I think I distracted him when I suggested we should make you dinner."

"Well, let me go see this masterpiece." She tipped her glass toward him and turned away.

He watched her go and reminded himself he should get ready to see her do that for real. To walk away and not come back.

It shouldn't matter that she would.

For some reason, though, it did matter.

———

LUCIE WAS TOO COMFORTABLE. SOME MUFFLED PART OF HER brain tried to nudge her to awareness, but as she sat on the sofa after dinner with Hayden beside her, pointing out silly characters in his book, it didn't seem important. She'd had a couple glasses of wine, a good meal, and the stress she'd felt in the first half of the day was gone. As if it never existed.

"Okay, buddy, story time is over."

Warmth slid along her veins at the deep, husky words, and she glanced over. Nate's dark gaze lingered on her face for a few seconds, and then his son climbed up to wrap his arms around her neck.

Startled, she hugged Hayden. "Good night," she whispered. "Sweet dreams."

He kissed her cheek. "You, too, Lucie." He released her, and then clambered over to his father, who hoisted him up as he rose.

She watched them go, then shut her eyes. She needed to distract herself.

"Hey."

She forced her eyes to open at his whisper.

Nate smiled a little. "Too much wine?"

"I don't think so. Just tired."

He leaned in and kissed her, and she opened for him without thinking.

Warmth washed over her, from his deep kiss, from his long fingers sliding into her hair, from the arm he wrapped around her to haul her onto his lap. When they surfaced a long time later, her only urge was *more*.

"Can I take you upstairs, Lucie?" he asked, his lips only a breath away from hers.

She nodded, unable to summon words.

He slid his arm beneath her legs and rose from the sofa, making her crazy pulse skip faster. She tightened her arms around his neck. "I've got you."

He certainly did, she realized, in more ways than one. If she wasn't careful, she'd fall for him.

When he put her down across his big bed a minute later, her heart thundered so loud in her ears, she couldn't hear the warnings. "Open," he ordered her, bending down to catch her mouth again.

She couldn't do anything else. Didn't want to do anything else.

She realized then she'd already fallen.

And she didn't want to do anything about it. Not now, with his rough hands carefully stroking over her, his warm mouth caressing her, his hard body buried deep inside her. Why would she?

Chapter Ten

L ucie jolted awake, her breath coming too fast.

"It's all right," Nate breathed just above her ear, one big hand flat on her belly.

"I have to go." Panic rushed through her. She could <u>not</u> be in love with him. She just couldn't.

His hold tightened. "Are you okay?" He sounded more awake now.

"Yes, I just have to go." She struggled to get her hand out from under the blankets.

"Lucie, take a breath. Did you have a bad dream?" His other hand stroked down her arm, gentle.

Her eyes burned, and she shook her head. "It's late. I can't stay." Holy shit, she really couldn't stay. Not now. She shoved upright, away from him.

The light clicked on from his side of the bed, and she squinted against the sudden brightness. "You're shaking."

She shook her head again. "I'm fine. Just realized how late it is." She didn't meet his gaze, turning away to hunt for her clothes.

The silence from behind her made her want to turn

around, but she didn't. Resolutely, she scrambled into her clothes, then dragged her fingers through her hair.

When she finally turned, Nate sat on the side of the bed, somber dark eyes locked on her face. "I didn't mean to scare you. Or wake you. I'm sorry."

His eyes narrowed slightly.

She bit her lip. "Go back to sleep, Nate." Her chest hurt, just looking at him. She was in so much trouble. She started for the door.

"Hang on."

Behind her, she heard soft rustling, and it took every ounce of her self-control not to turn. "I'll lock the door behind me. You should stay in bed." She closed her fingers on the doorknob.

Half a second later, his fingers settled on her shoulder. "Look at me, Lucie."

She winced, then took a quick breath and tried to school her expression to something like normal before she lifted her face.

His mouth turned down a little as he studied her. "I'll walk you down if you really insist on going," he said after a few seconds.

She nodded and turned the doorknob.

He remained silent while she hurried into her coat, though he eased her hair free of the hood while she fumbled the zipper up. Then he set his hands on both sides of her face and stepped closer.

Some of her inner alarm must have shown in her eyes, because the corners of his mouth turned further down. She took a shallow breath and reached up with one hand to touch his cheek. "I'm okay, Nate. Really."

"You're a terrible liar," he said flatly. Still, he bent to brush a kiss on her mouth. "Keys?"

She stuck her free hand in her pocket, and came up empty. She pulled her other hand from his face and stuck into the other pocket. Nothing. "Shit."

Nate stepped back, frowning.

She fumbled through the inside pockets of her coat, and then jammed her hands into her jeans pockets. No keys. Of all the times to lose her keys...

"Maybe they fell out upstairs. I'll look."

"I'll check the living room." She retraced her steps into the other room and started pulling cushions from the couch. *Nothing.* Panic threaded along her veins again. She never left the house without double-checking to be sure she had her keys. Now she struggled to think back–had she been in such a rush to get things together and leave with Hayden that she'd failed to do her double-check?

Maybe.

She put the last cushion back on the sofa and looked up at a soft jingle.

Nate descended the last few steps, with her keys dangling from his forefinger.

Relief rushed after the panic, making her light-headed for a second. "Thank you," she whispered.

He smiled a little. "Lost in the blankets." He tucked them into her pocket and tugged her closer again to kiss her, hard. "You should stay." His fingers squeezed her hips once.

"What would Hayden think?"

His smile faded, and one of his shoulders jerked in a shrug. "I think he'd be okay."

"But what if he isn't?" She reached up to touch his mouth, lightly. "I can't do that." Not to Hayden, or to herself. She couldn't.

Nate kissed her again, softer. "If you're sure."

She nodded, feeling a lump gather in her throat.

"So we'll see you in the morning." His fingers stroked once more.

"Okay," she managed, and stepped away from him.

After she'd gotten into her own house, she leaned against the closed door for a long minute, gulping in air to try to dislodge the tears trying to clog her airway. She'd fallen in love with him. She knew better. Dammit, even if she wasn't only staying here temporarily, she couldn't do this again.

———

NATE DIDN'T LIKE THE LOOK IN LUCIE'S EYES IN THE morning, or the dark smudges beneath them, as though she hadn't slept at all after she left his bed last night. He didn't like the way she avoided his gaze to greet his son. Or her too-easy agreement when he said he wanted to take Hayden over to see his parents around lunchtime. She seemed almost relieved.

That stung, he mused as he finished assembling the sink cabinet for his current job. And made him wonder again what had frightened her awake last night. He moved on to the next cabinet, pondering. The only thing he could come up with by the time he'd finished the rest of the cabinets was that the idea of taking on the restaurant had scared the hell out of her.

He'd pushed too hard.

He should apologize when he picked Hayden up.

He forgot all about that, though, when she opened the door for him, and she was dressed up. He blinked at her knee-length green skirt, black boots, and white blouse. "You look very nice."

Pink tinted her cheeks. "Thank you."

"You have an interview?" he guessed, his gut clenching.

She nodded. "I had a message waiting last night, so I

called back this morning, and we're having an informal chat this afternoon."

He wanted to say the right thing. 'That's great.' 'Good for you.' 'You'll do great.' But he couldn't force himself to say the words. "Oh," was all he could manage.

She bit her lip as she met his gaze for a second, hers guarded.

"Hey, Daddy! You should see our puzzle." Hayden wrapped one arm around his leg.

"Oh yeah?" He shifted his attention from Lucie to Hayden.

His son nodded vigorously. "It's a buncha flowers, an' they're all the same. It's hard."

Nate smiled. "I bet. Well, we should get out of Lucie's way so she can go, and so you can see Grandpa. He's probably ready for you." He looked at her again, but she was smiling down at his son.

"We'll see you for supper, Lucie," Hayden said as he pulled his coat onto one arm.

Her smile faded. "Okay. Have a good time, buddy."

Nate's stomach sank. She was really going to go. He reached out automatically to help his son with his coat, and she stepped back, out of reach, to pick up Hayden's hat.

"Be careful," he said. "The road might be slick between here and the ferry."

She faked a smile. "I will, thanks." She bent to slip the hat onto his son's head.

Hayden gave her a quick hug. "See you later, Lucie." He ran for the door.

Nate hesitated, but the cold air that blasted them forced him to follow his son out. He didn't know what to say. He reached back to pull the door shut, catching a glimpse of the sadness in her green eyes before the door swung between them.

Dammit.

He'd fucked this up somehow. He knew that, he just didn't know what he'd done or how to undo it.

It dogged him all afternoon, through lunch with his parents, while chatting with his parents as Hayden napped, on the drive home. Lucie's car wasn't back when he pulled into the driveway, and the house was dark, not even the front porch light on to help her find her way.

He turned on his own porch lights, front and back, once he'd gotten Hayden inside. It occurred to him, though, that she might not actually come over to his house. Not tonight.

He wondered what time her interview had been. Where? If he'd thought to ask earlier, he would have a better idea when she'd be home.

And she hadn't offered the information.

Nate stared out the back door, rubbing one hand in the middle of his chest. He didn't have any right to ask, really. He had nothing to tempt her to stay on the island. They had agreed this was temporary.

Fuck it, he didn't want it to be temporary.

His breath rushed out. He didn't have any business thinking like that. He had a son to consider. Relationships were too messy, especially with kids involved.

Another flash of realization—<u>she</u> already knew that.

God, he was an idiot.

———

Lucie eased her car into the dark driveway. Lights blazed next door, and her chest squeezed. It was way past suppertime, something she hadn't planned directly, but something that had been in the back of her mind when she left the island earlier.

The interview had gone well. Another training writing position. Nothing she was excited about.

But it was practical.

Not nearly as practical, though, was her visit to the office of her investment company, where she'd been putting all the money she'd saved while working her practical jobs up to this point. The stop had been a whim when she left the interview. Just to see what options she might have, if she decided to be impractical.

The restaurant on the island was far more doable than she'd realized.

A location off-island would probably not be as easily achieved, unless she found another equally motivated seller.

But buying this one meant staying on the island and seeing Nate and Hayden.

She wasn't sure she could do that.

Sighing, she stepped out of the car and into the brisk air coming in from the bluff. She should have left a porch light on earlier. She fumbled for the door key in her pocket, and managed to get it into the lock, shivering when she stepped inside, out of the cold.

Leaning against the closed door, she focused on forcing some of the tension from her muscles. It took a few minutes, but eventually, she felt slightly better and pushed off the door, flipping on a lamp on the end table just inside the door. It wasn't nearly time for bed, she mused, but she was ready to curl up in bed right now, to not think anymore tonight.

Then her stomach growled.

Sighing, she slipped her coat off and carried it into the dark kitchen to hang beside the door.

The tap at the back door made her jump.

She turned on the porch light, but didn't see anyone. She stepped closer, and then saw the top of Hayden's blond head. <u>Uh-oh.</u> Frowning, she turned on the overhead light in the kitchen as she opened the door.

"Hey, buddy, are you all right?"

"You didn't come home for supper."

Her heart squeezed. "I'm sorry. It took me longer in the city than I thought it would."

He stepped inside. "You should come."

"You didn't have supper yet?" She dropped to her knees beside him, pushing the door shut to keep out the wind. "And you don't have your heavy coat on."

"I just wanted to come get you."

"Does your dad know you're here?"

He looked down at his feet.

She sighed. "Oh, Hayden." Reluctantly, she pushed to her feet and took her coat from the hook. "Let's get you back over to your house before your dad has a heart attack." Never mind that her own heart was pounding like crazy at just the thought of going over there.

When they stepped onto the patio, she heard a door slam.

"Hayden!"

"He's here," she called, hearing her voice shake.

Nate came at a run, fear and relief shadowing his expression. "Hayden, you scared me." He squatted in front of the little boy. "Why did you leave the house without talking to me first?"

"I just wanted Lucie to come over," he said quietly.

Nate's head bowed for a moment, and then he released a quick breath. "It's time for you to get ready for bed, buddy."

Her ribs squeezed. He hadn't even looked at her.

"Lucie hasta come."

She swallowed. *Now...*

"Okay."

She blinked as he rose. But...

Hayden beamed up at her, and she bit her tongue. She couldn't argue. Not when he looked so happy.

The three of them trooped across the backyard in silence, through the gate, and into Nate's mud room. Hayden let his dad take his light jacket off, then he ran ahead into the house.

Nate turned to her, his expression unreadable in the dark mud room. "How did your interview go?"

She tightened her fingers on the edges of her coat. "Okay. She wants to set up a formal interview with the hiring committee."

He grunted and caught the collar of her coat.

She let him take it, stifling a shiver when his fingers brushed her nape.

"Read my story, Lucie!" Hayden shouted from the living room.

She hesitated, then moved away from Nate, fixing a smile on her face when she emerged into the kitchen. Hayden clambered onto the sofa with his book, and she sat beside him. Nate followed more slowly, dropping onto the sofa on the other side of his son.

"Read, Lucie."

She took the book, daring a quick peek over at the silent man. His attention was on his son. Taking a slow breath, she opened the book and started to read.

The little boy cuddled against her side, and her chest ached. By the time the story was over, his eyes drooped.

"Come on, buddy," Nate said softly, scooping up his son.

As he rose, Lucie closed the book and shifted forward on the couch.

He leveled a stern look at her. "Stay."

Her mouth went dry, so she swallowed, then nodded. She

sat there when he went upstairs, listening to the soft creak of the floor in Hayden's room.

She shouldn't be here. She wasn't at all sure she could keep from blurting out something stupid. Or bursting into tears. It was ridiculous.

She shoved to her feet, then froze when she heard his footfalls on the stairs.

"Did you eat?"

She shook her head.

"Come on. We had some leftover spaghetti and meatballs and Hayden wanted to save you some."

Her stomach pitched. "I'm not hungry," she whispered.

He studied her face for a long moment. "Okay. Why don't you sit down? You're pale."

"Hayden scared me." She dropped onto the front edge of the sofa again, knees weak.

"Me, too." Nate nudged the coffee table away, then sat on it, facing her. "So the hiring committee sounds promising. What's the job?"

She bowed her head to look at her hands. "The same thing I was doing at my last job."

"Practical."

His flat tone made her glance up, but she forced herself to stop at his chin. "I guess."

"So you're set on that, huh?"

The backs of her eyes burned. "No, not really."

He caught her hands. "Lucie."

"I'm sorry about Hayden."

"Lucie." He tightened his fingers around hers a little.

She licked her lower lip and dragged her gaze a bit higher.

"I don't want you to go."

"Nate, I don't think I can do casual or temporary," she

choked out. "And Hayden..." She bit her lip, blinking against the stinging in her eyes.

He released one of her hands to brush her cheek, and she realized a tear had slid down her face. "I don't think I'm good at temporary either." A ghost of a smile touched his mouth. "Don't cry, Lucie. I'm doing a terrible job saying this. I want you to stay here. With us."

She felt the next few tears burn down her cheeks.

He leaned in and brushed a kiss on her mouth. "Don't cry, sweetheart."

She bit her lip again, but the sob still escaped.

Nate pulled her closer. "I hope that isn't you wanting to tell me you're leaving. I need you, Lucie. You're the best thing that's happened to me in a long time."

She buried her face in his soft shirt, stuffing her fist against her mouth. She shook with the effort to contain her tears.

Nate gathered her closer, closer, until she was on his lap, one of his big hands sliding up and down her spine, soothing. He whispered into her hair, incomprehensible words, his tone low.

It took her a long time to master the tears, and she rubbed one hand over her face. "I'm sorry, Nate."

"Hopefully just that my shirt is soaked through, and not 'sorry, Nate, I'm leaving'."

She tipped her head back to look up at him. "The first one," she whispered.

The tight line of his jaw relaxed a tiny bit.

"I actually went somewhere else after my interview," she started.

He waited.

"While I worked my practical jobs, I saved money for 'someday'. I don't know what for. Anyway, I stopped to talk to someone at the office there about this restaurant idea."

His fingers tightened on her.

"Turns out I can probably afford to pull this off."

"But?"

"But I don't want to do it if...if we are just temporary." The last word was barely audible.

Nate smiled, slow and wide. "Really?"

She nodded once.

"Good thing I don't want us to be temporary."

She sucked in an unsteady breath. "I don't know what's got into me. I've never been so rash and reckless before." She sniffed a little.

"Island air." He leaned in and brushed another kiss on her mouth. "You'll stay?"

"I think I have to. I'm in love with you."

He went still for a moment, then crushed her to his chest, his face against her hair. "I didn't expect to feel like this, Lucie, not ever again. You've ruined my good intentions."

She laughed, sliding her hand around his back. "We're both crazy, right? Who falls in love like this?"

"Evidently we do." He eased back enough to kiss her. Softly, lingering.

Lucie relaxed in his arms, all of the tension and fear from the last twenty-four hours vanishing.

"You're staying tonight, right?" he asked when he released her mouth at last.

"But Hayden..." She stopped at the look in his eyes. "Maybe."

The hard line of his mouth softened again. "I love you, too, Lucie."

Her eyes burned all over again.

"I hope those are good tears." He nudged her nose with his.

She nodded. "I just didn't think this was happening." She swallowed. "Are you sure, Nate?"

He tipped her chin up so he could catch her gaze. "Positive."

Her pulse skipped at the intensity in his eyes. "Holy shit. Pinch me."

He obliged, pinching her butt, gently. "Real," he murmured, leaning in to kiss her again.

Lucie kissed him back, withholding nothing. Her emotions welled up, spilled over.

Nate soothed her, stroking her back, her cheek, her scalp. Gentle. Until she didn't want to be soothed anymore. Then he roused her need, stroking all of the spots that made her hot, aroused her so she squirmed in his lap.

And then he pressed her under him on the couch, scrambling to dislodge enough clothing to bury himself inside her.

She whimpered each time he withdrew, bit her lip at the pleasure every time he thrust back inside her. And the release rushed up before she was ready.

"I love you, Lucie," he growled, catching her mouth, his body quaking over hers.

She smiled into the kiss.

Epilogue

Light footsteps rushed down the steps, and Lucie smiled when Hayden stopped in the middle of the living room.

"Good morning, buddy."

"Whatcha doin', Lucie?"

"I'm making French toast for breakfast." She glanced down at her sweater and leggings. She'd only just gotten back from her place, after getting a quick shower and dressing in fresh clothes.

"I like French toast." He padded into the kitchen.

"I thought you might." She dropped the last egg into the bowl and started to whisk them together.

"Hey, there."

She glanced up when Nate came down the last couple of steps. He was also freshly showered, his hair still wet. He grinned at her, making her cheeks heat.

Hayden looked back at his father. "How come Lucie's makin' breakfast?"

"Lucie and I wanted to ask what you'd think about Lucie staying here with us forever."

Blue eyes widened, and he turned to Lucie again, while she held her breath. "Really? You'd stay with us?"

"I would," she managed, setting the bowl and whisk on the counter.

"Woohoo!" He ran at her, wrapping his arms around her legs. "Really? Forever?"

"Forever," she whispered, watching his father approach.

"I like forever," Hayden said, unwrapping one arm from her leg to hug Nate's leg, too. "I'm glad Mr. Micah brought you here for us, Lucie."

Nate leaned in to brush a kiss on her mouth. "Me, too."

About the Author

Elizabeth Andrews has been a book lover since she was old enough to read. She read her copies of *Little Women* and the *Little House* series so many times, the books fell apart. As an adult, her book habit continues. She has a room overflowing with her literary collection right now, and still more spreading into other rooms. Almost as long as she's been reading great stories, she's been attempting to write her own. Thanks to a fifth grade teacher who started the class on creative writing, Elizabeth went from writing creative sentences to short stories and eventually full-length novels. Her father saved her poor, callused fingers from permanent damage when he brought home a used typewriter for her.

Elizabeth found her mother's stash of romance novels as a teenager, and-though she loves horror- romance became her very favorite genre, making writing romances a natural progression. There are more than just a few manuscripts, however, tucked away in a filing cabinet that will never see the light of day.

Along with her enormous book stash, Elizabeth lives with her husband of more than twenty years, with frequent visits to and from her two young adult sons. When she's not at work or buried in books or writing, there is a garden outside full of herbs, flowers and vegetables that requires occasional attention.

You can visit her website to learn more: www.elizabethandrewswrites.com